THE CANTOR

A LEGION OF PNEUMOS NOVELLA

H.B. RENEAU

VESALIAN PUBLISHING

Acknowledgments

This book wouldn't have been possible without the help and input of family, friends, roommates, classmates, editors, and beta readers.

Special thanks go to my editor Lara Kennedy, whose insight and guidance helped turn this manuscript into the finished product before you. Thank you also to Natalia Junqueira for her gorgeous cover design.

"Writing is like driving at night. You can see only as far as the head-lights, but you can make the whole trip that way."
– E.L. Doctorow

Thank you all for believing in the road ahead.

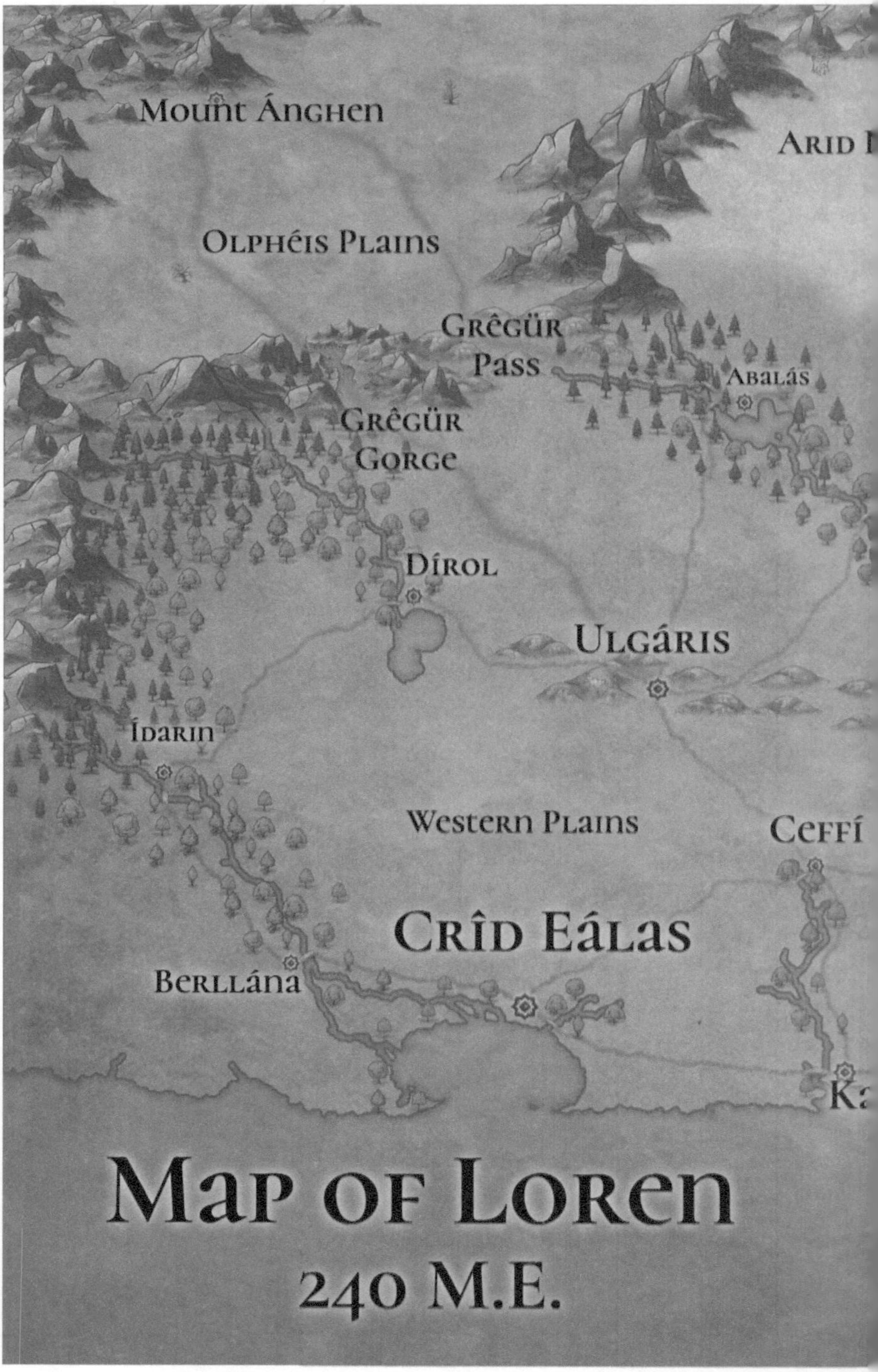
Mount Ánghen
Arid
Olphéis Plains
Grêgür Pass
Abalás
Grêgür Gorge
Dírol
Ulgáris
Ídarin
Western Plains
Ceffí
Crîd Eálas
Berllána
Map of Loren
240 M.E.

the North
Port Tuálath
Port Cála
Port alaén
Fertile Inlet
Eastern Plains
Port Mârfa
a
Southern Shield
Tibolé

PROLOGUE

Rain on glass, windshield breaks
Screeching tires. Headlights.
Screaming, prayers, and crying. Pain.

Keira ran, crashing through the forest, branches grabbing at her hair and tearing at her clothes. She blinked tears out of her eyes as she collapsed heavily against an old oak, clutching it as she tried desperately to gulp down air.

Instead, she vomited nothing but bile.

She wiped her mouth with the back of her hand and straightened, shielding her eyes to see through the dense forest. Where were they?

She ran, the flashes of memory coming unbidden.

Rain. Tires. Headlights.

She stumbled, her foot stubbing against a half-buried root with a sharp pang that coursed up her leg. Her knee raked against a jagged stone as she fell. The urge to scream rose, catching in her throat. She bit her lip to quell it. Digging her nails into the moist earth, she felt the tears fall unhindered.

I have to find them.

They'd been on their way to campus, car loaded with everything a girl might need for her first year at college. It'd been raining, and she'd nodded off to the sound of Molly's excited questioning and her mother's patient responses, only waking when the car slammed into the rail. Keira fought down the rising panic at the thought of her mother and little Molly, always like a sister to her. She swallowed, the memories coming hard and fast now. They'd hydroplaned, spinning in circles. She remembered the shine of oncoming headlights refracted in rainbow arrays through the raindrops on the windshield. There'd been a crash, metal on metal, then stillness and the sickening feeling of falling. Down, down, down they went.

Screaming. Crying. Pain.

She had to find them. *Now.* They could be hurt or worse and they *needed* her. But where was she? Where were the others? Had she somehow been thrown from the car? But she'd been wearing her seatbelt, hadn't she? She couldn't see any road from here and thought she might barf again. She closed her eyes and leaned her face against cool earth, hand clutching reflexively at the locket that still hung from her neck as she listened to the sound of running water.

Water!

Hadn't they driven over a river last night? Keira thought they might have, but she couldn't be sure. Her brain felt fuzzy around the edges. *I have to get to the water*, she decided. An icy drink would do her good, at the very least. There had to be somebody, anybody, who would help her find them. She lurched to her feet and tried to run again, but her wounded knee was having none of it. So she limped as fast as she could in the sound's direction. She saw stars and grasped wildly at trunks and vegetation, lurching from side to side as her balance faltered. Finally, she emerged into a clearing.

The river she'd heard before ran right through it, and she could just make out smoke in the distance. Then she saw him, a lone figure standing at the river's edge, shading his eyes as he gazed across at her.

Oh, thank God!

She tried to call out and wave her arms. But her voice was a raspy croak, almost inaudible, and her legs seemed unwilling to move even the shortest distance. Her knees buckled, and she braced herself against a tree. He must have seen her, though, as he quickly sheathed the sword he'd held at the ready. Wait, a *sword*? She really must have hit her head. But yes, she was sure now that it was a *he*, as the sun glinted off his tall frame and cropped, sandy-colored hair.

He was walking toward her now, hands outstretched, as if approaching a deer that might bolt at any second. Keira didn't feel capable of bolting anywhere at the moment. Her head swam and black specks colored her vision. The weight of her head seemed enormous, and she thought briefly about how much she'd like to lie down.

He was saying something now. His mouth was moving, but her ears felt stuffed with cotton balls, and she couldn't make out the words.

She felt herself sway and half-decided, half-conceded to plop to the ground. Her hand flew to her chest and caught the locket there, just as she felt the weight of it loosen around her neck. She stared down at the piece of gold as if another hand held it, its broken clasp glinting in the sunlight. Another wave of vertigo hit her and she let herself sway to the side, catching herself before her head hit the ground. She was perfectly happy to lie there, willing the world to stop spinning. The man ran toward her now, brow furrowed in concern. *Strange.* Exhaustion washed over her, and she closed her eyes.

CHAPTER

ONE

Six Hours Earlier

"MOM! Have you seen my yellow sweater?"

Buried elbow deep in an overflowing chest of drawers and face screwed into a tight grimace, Keira Altman furiously tossed items into an old suitcase—wheels scuffed and corners fraying from use. As the minutes passed, her movements grew more harried, the various articles of clothing strewn about the room evidence enough of her anxious search.

Computer, coat, textbooks. Keira mentally ran through the list of items on her packing list, a mantra that kept her pulse to a dull throb in her ears. *Where is that dang sweater?*

A small *click* from the doorway caught her attention and Keira glanced up to find her mother perched in the doorway. Tammy Altman's dark curls spilled out of her hastily set top knot as she waved the developing Polaroid in a fluttering motion, as though settling fairy dust around the room.

"Just waiting for the magic," she said, grinning widely. Keira couldn't help but return the smile, the shared joke a running thread throughout her childhood. After a few moments, Tammy held the photo out to admire her handiwork.

"Ahh," her mother sighed. "Just beautiful, baby."

Keira blushed and tucked her own dark curls behind one ear self-consciously, but took the photo and added it to the stack as she resumed taking down the polaroid collage from the wall above her bed. The arrangement was a tangible reminder of all the homes and places she and her mother had inhabited over the last 17 years, and the ritual of confining it to boxes for temporary relocation felt oddly comforting.

"So many adventures," her mother sighed, draping an arm across Keira's shoulders as she inspected the wall. "Nothing at all like *my* childhood." She snorted derisively and Keira smiled tightly in response. She knew all about her mother's sedentary childhood on a small farm in rural Kansas, had heard countless times how much happier her mother was now that she was free to roam and explore the world. Keira suspected the distance from her mother's abusive alcoholic father played no small part in this desire.

For her part, Keira wouldn't have minded just a bit more sedentary. After all, fourteen schools in twelve years was a lot for any kid to handle. At this point, Keira was an expert at being the new kid and practically had a degree in Relocation 101. Not that she'd tell her mother any of that. Tammy had enough on her plate.

"Oh baby, you're gonna have such a wonderful time at college. You'll have good friends, exciting parties, and so many stories to share. Just try not to study *too* much." Tammy added, pressing a finger teasingly to Keira's nose. "And watch out for those boys. You know what I always say. They're nice to look at but you can't trust any of them when the you-know-what hits the fan."

Keira rolled her eyes. "I know Mom." Honestly, after seeing her mother's experiences flitting from one new boyfriend to the next, each more down on his luck than the last, romance was the absolute last thing on her mind. But something else hummed at the forefront.

College, Keira thought. The word sent a flurry of fear and excitement racing through her limbs. Four years in one place. Just the thought of it sent a nervous thrill through her. Would she make friends? Could she even keep friends for that long? She'd never had the chance to try.

A sudden wave of panic rushed over her and Keira took a deep, unsteady breath. What was she doing? For as long as she could remember, it had just been her and her mother. Tammy hadn't been much older than Keira herself when she'd gotten pregnant and it had always been the two of them against the world. Could Keira really do this on her own?

"Maybe I should have gone somewhere closer," Keira whispered, wrapping an arm around her mother's waist.

"Ahh, it's gonna be fine baby," Tammy crooned, pulling Keira more tightly against her shoulder. "You're only a couple of hours away. We'll see each other all the time."

"You promise?" Keira whispered, hating how small she sounded in that moment, but needing the reassurance nonetheless.

"Cross my heart," her mother murmured and Keira could hear the smile in her voice. Keira roughly swiped an arm across her face and steadied herself.

"Well," she said, tapping both hands against her knees as she propelled herself up from the bed. "I can't go anywhere until I track down that sweater. It's lucky you know." Keira grinned over at her mother, expecting some teasing response about how Altmans made their own luck. Instead, her mother grimaced, biting her lip as she scuffed one slipper against the floor.

"Sooo, I think I found it."

From her tone, Keira braced herself for disappointment. Tammy Altman had never been the most reliable of mothers. Whether it was missed school pickups, forgotten lunches, or the whims of her latest boyfriend. Tammy had always lived her life tossed and turned by a sea of flippant moods. One day she'd be all excitement, upbeat and ready to take on the day, and on the next she'd be barely able to drag herself from her bed. Most days, Keira didn't mind. After all, her mother's airy presence had turned many a rainy day into a splashing hunt for fairies in the garden and her mystical thinking had shaped every hasty eviction into a fantasy quest, a foray into the thrilling unknown.

But when it came to practical matters and the daily necessities of living, Keira had long ago learned to lower her expectations of her mother. Normally she took these minor inconveniences in stride, knowing Tammy never did it on purpose. On the average day Keira would already be three steps ahead, anticipation of her mother's lapses yielding proactive preparation.

Today was not one of those days.

"Sooooo, I was doing laundry, and you know how I get so distracted. It's really not the best chore for me..."

Keira pursed her lips, shoving down her annoyance at the insinuation that this was somehow *her* fault.

"...and I maaaay have thrown it into the dryer."

From the laundry basket in the hall, Tammy pulled the shrunken remains of Keira's favorite yellow sweater, the pilling bunching into clumps that threatened to unravel the already frayed edges.

Keira smoothed her face into one of casual indifference, blinking away the sting of tears and hiding the disappointment that bloomed to the surface. It was silly to get so upset over a sweater, even if it was her go-to first day of school outfit.

I don't need it, she told herself. *It's college. Everyone will be new.*

"It's fine," she said thinly and turned to fold the rest of the clothes into the waiting boxes.

"I'm so sorry, baby. I know you loved that sweater. But I got you something and I think you're *really* going to like it."

Keira forced her lips into a smile as she said, "Oh yeah? You didn't have to do that, Mom. I know money's been tight this month and you still need to get your alternator replaced . . ."

Tammy waved her concerns away with the flick of one wrist, and Keira suppressed another wave of panic. Forget her worries about college. How would her mother cope with being on her own? Keira had already made a list of all the bills and their due dates and pinned them to the fridge, but what would happen during the next move? Keira had better save a copy to her computer so that—

". . . know you're not much of a jewelry person but I thought you'd enjoy having a little piece of home."

Keira forced herself to focus on her mother's words and put aside her growing to-do list. *She'll be fine,* Keira told herself. *She's a grown woman.* But though she forced a smile on her face, Keira was far from convinced.

With a flourish, Tammy withdrew a long golden locket from one pocket. Keira stared at it, taken aback as the light glinted off its gilded edges.

"Oh Mom," Keira breathed. "It's beautiful."

"Isn't it? Old Sal down at the flea market robbed me blind but I decided it was more than worth it for my baby's first at college. Go on now, open it."

Keira glanced sideways, but ignored her mother's flippant comment. Instead, she took the locket gently and popped the clasp to open it. Inside was a picture of Keira and her mother when Keira was no more than six or seven, if the number of missing front teeth were any indication. Opposite bore the inscription, "Though she be but little, she is fierce."

"A Midsummer Night's Dream," Keira murmured.

"I always did fancy myself a Hermia," Tammy declared, fluttering her arms theatrically. Keira snorted and shook her head, but didn't take her eyes away from the beautiful locket. She'd never wanted for the essentials growing up. Despite her flighty nature, Tammy possessed the uncanny ability to acquire any needed funds at the eleventh hour, no matter the direness of straights. But luxuries like this had always been so beyond Keira's experience that she wouldn't even have known to want them.

"Thank you, Mom." Keira murmured, smiling up at her mother as she fastened the necklace around her neck. "I love it."

"I knew you would. Now," Tammy declared, "put me to work. It's time we got on the road and you know Molly will be fit to bursting with questions by the time we pick her up."

Keira rolled her eyes but passed her mother a cardboard box. Molly was the eight-year-old daughter of Tammy's friend Didi, a fellow waitress at the local diner and best described as a more absent-minded version of Tammy—if such a thing could be imagined. Her daughter Molly was curious about everything and loved books almost as much as Keira had at that age. Keira was her go-to babysitter and given the hours that both moms worked, Molly had become something like a little sister. It had been Keira's idea to take her with them on their drive to Stanford. She wanted Molly to see what college was like—the future she might have if she worked hard and did well in school. She may not have the advantages of a stable home like most kids, but Keira was convinced that if she could do it, then so could Molly.

"I'm almost finished with the clothes, so that just leaves the books."

"Ugh," Tammy groaned aloud. "Good thing you'll be a doctor someday baby, my poor back will need a replacement from years hauling around the mountain that is your book collection."

Keira rolled her eyes and resumed folding. "They don't replace backs, Mom."

"Not now, they don't," Tammy replied, winking conspiratorially. "You'll just have to be the first one."

Keira laughed aloud and the two of them finished the packing. As Keira loaded the last of the boxes into their small hatchback, she could almost forget the flutter of butterflies in her stomach.

A new start, she thought to herself. *Just what I need.*

CHAPTER

TWO

As a general rule, Danny O'Leary didn't place much stock in dreams, portents, or any other such nonsense. But waking up in a cold sweat to the sound of screams would be a doozy for anyone.

He lay there for a long moment amidst twisted and damp sheets, chest heaving in the pre-dawn darkness. He could still hear the screams and the shriek of tires on wet pavement along with the sickening sensation of dropping. Danny shook his head, shoving the memory as far from his mind as possible—which was to say, not very far at all.

"Come on then, get a grip." Danny muttered, turning from one side and then the next as he searched in vain for the sleep that eluded him. He really didn't need this. Not after the doozy that was last night. Finally, he sighed in defeat. Clearly, he would not find his way to sleep tonight.

So roughly pulling on his boots and quietly padded out of his room, down the tightly spiraling wood staircase, and outside to the stables. His horse, Boyd, nickered softly to him as he lit the lantern, nuzzling his arm with his long snout.

"Ay, boy-o," Danny cooed softly at his palomino gelding, stroking a knuckle between the horse's wide eyes. He inhaled deeply the scent of damp hay and earth, letting the chilly air fill his nostrils and clear his senses. And as the last dregs of sleep fled his mind, the memory of last night's fight immediately stole its place.

He winced. Things really had gotten out of hand. It all started by an offhand comment Nazor had made to Elliott about the annual gathering, when Legionnaires from across Loren would gather to discuss the state of order and their efforts to keep the peace.

I'm excited to see Port Galaén, Danny had said. *I've heard there's really nothin' quite like it.*

His mentors had exchanged a glance at that.

What? Danny had asked.

Nazor snorted. *You'll be staying here, Danny. Same as last year. The gathering is for legionnaires only.*

But I'm ready, Danny had protested. *It's been a year now. A year of training and preparation. I'm ready for the rites.*

You know why you must wait, Danny. Elliott had said kindly. *Until your cantor arrives, there's a whole facet of Legionnaire training you've yet to complete.*

Danny had rolled his eyes at that. Ah yes, this mysterious cantor. He'd waited a whole year for this mysterious partner, this other half, who was the key to unlocking his true abilities. Fat load of good all that waiting had gotten him.

Then where the bloody hell are they? He'd demanded. *If they're so important, then why aren't they here? Hell, why am I here?*

Watch your tone, Nazor growled.

He'd shoved away from the dinner table after that, in no mood for whatever patient explanation Elliott had in store.

In the harsh light of day, guilt gnawed at him for his unkind words. That wasn't him. Danny was normally the levelheaded one. He'd always been that way. Quicker to watch and wait than jump in headfirst to any sort of scrum. But he was tired. He'd arrived almost a year ago now and he missed his home and his family. And what's more, he was no closer to understanding why he'd been brought to this strange world in the first place. But that was no excuse for rudeness.

He quickly pushed the memory away. No use dwelling on it now. He'd apologize to Nazor and Elliott when he got the chance. But until then, there was work to be done. He shivered lightly in the predawn chill as he set about his usual morning chores, grateful for the distraction. He moved with practiced skill, his hands and feet setting to work seemingly without direction. It wasn't until he was halfway done mucking out the stalls that he realized that in his distracted state, he'd sped through them in record time.

"Not bad for an Irish city boy," he chuckled to himself, pushing the sandy locks off his sweating brow. "If Mam could only see me now."

A stab of pain cut through him, and he realized with a start that he hadn't thought of his mother in months, nor his three little sisters and the shabby flat they'd shared in South Boston.

Danny found he could barely remember his father, the textile mill worker who'd died of tuberculosis when Danny was nine, not long after the Depression was in full swing. Luckily for them, Danny's family had an aunt and uncle who'd let the family move in. He'd been able to remain in school (largely at his mother's insistence), but it wasn't long before he started working long hours in his uncle's grocery whenever he could to help take care of his mother and sisters. As Danny got older, his uncle had seen he had a talent for figures and so had put him to work managing stock and shipments. Eventually, his uncle let him take an even larger role in managing the business, grooming him to one day take over the grocery itself.

That was all put on hold one day in December, when the Japs attacked Pearl Harbor and America decided that maybe Germany and its cronies weren't just somebody else's problem. Danny had just turned eighteen, so he, along with most every other boy he knew, had enlisted straight off.

His mother was beside herself and begged him not to go. Danny could still remember the tears streaming down her cheeks as she pleaded with him. But if there was one thing Danny understood, it was the importance of duty and fulfilling one's responsibilities. He was doing this for his family, as surely as he had worked every day since the age of nine to care for them.

Sure, maybe there was a small part of him that relished the adventure, that thrilled at the thought of getting out of Boston and seeing what else there was in the world, but he was no fool. He didn't believe for one moment that the old war stories of glory and heroism were anything more than the long-embellished memories of Great War veterans who sought meaning in why they had to come home far more broken than when they'd left. Danny may not have known exactly what awaited him in Europe, but he also knew that he was needed, and that settled the matter. It had been years since he'd seen his family, since he'd joined the army and left home to fight a war on a far-off continent he knew little about. It was just under a year ago now. He'd woken up after a lucky sniper round and found himself suddenly in Loren, a world far stranger than he ever could have imagined. Nazor and Elliott had tried to make their farm feel like home to him, and in a way, it did. But every once in a while, thoughts of his old life and the world he'd left behind crept in.

With the chores seen to, Danny went back inside the old stone house to find Elliott and Nazor already seated at the table, enjoying their breakfast.

"You're up early," Elliott commented. "Trouble sleeping?"

Danny shrugged and took the seat next to Nazor. Never one for much chitchat before noon, she said nothing and merely passed him the bread and cheese board. He glanced at her, waiting for any sign of coldness or disapproval after their recent spat. But there was nothing. Nazor wasn't one to hold grudges. Danny felt the tension in his back loosen as he settled himself more comfortably on the bench.

"I had another one of those dreams," he told Elliott, who glanced up in surprise. "I still can't make it all out," Danny said hurriedly, "but I'm fairly sure it involves some sort of car accident."

"Oh?" Elliott asked, leaning forward slightly. Danny shook his head. Having died in the late 1870s, Elliott found any reference to futuristic technology, such as cars and telephones, inexplicably thrilling.

"Yeah, and the thing is, well, there was this girl, and there's just something about her . . ." Danny looked up from the small loaf he was turning over in his hands to see them both gazing curiously at him. "Well, for starters, she died."

Elliott choked on his juice. Nazor said nothing, but Danny saw her eyes widen, and she put down the apple she'd been about to take a bite out of.

"What happened?" she asked quietly, seeing that Elliott was still clearing his throat.

Danny eyed the older woman cautiously. It was times like these when he depended on her steadiness. Sure, she could be intimidating, but she was also the first person he'd go to for advice or help. Elliott always meant well, but there was no telling what he'd do or say if Danny tried to explain the strange connection he'd felt to this girl and the sense of devastation when he'd realized she was gone.

So, resolving to give the full story to Nazor later, he shrugged and said only, "There was a car accident. They went off the road on the side of a mountain. There's no way anyone survived that." Danny swallowed, feeling Nazor's dark eyes on him, searching his face with her oddly knowing gaze.

"How terrible," Elliott breathed.

Danny could feel his intent gaze and glanced away, making his own face an unreadable mask before it betrayed him.

"But you know," Elliott continued, considering, "this could be what we've been waiting for."

Danny shot him a look and said, perhaps a little too sharply, "What's that supposed to mean?"

Elliott seemed not to notice Danny's change in tone, for he merely continued, "Danny, we talked before about how these were very unlikely to be normal dreams. This girl most likely exists somewhere. It's been nearly a year since you arrived here in Loren, and we've yet to hear of your counterpart turning up anywhere in this region. Perhaps that's why you keep having this dream. She may very well be your *cantor*."

Danny froze, feeling the twin twinges of excitement and nervousness dueling for dominance in his head. Sure, the possibility of his wayward partner's long-awaited arrival excited him. And yet, the relationship between grounder and cantor, although ideally represented by Elliott and Nazor, was still something of a mystery to him. He knew that high-level pneumonancy required this relationship. To be wielded properly, pneuma must be both cast out and grounded to a single spot. Yet the relationship he saw between Elliott and Nazor seemed to be something far more ethereal that he just didn't truly understand. That said, it *would* explain the strange connection he'd felt with the curly-haired girl that kept appearing in his dreams. He would readily admit that the idea of her not being truly dead, but only in transition, was certainly comforting.

"Do you think we should postpone your trip to Port Galaén just in case? We'll be headed there for the gathering in the spring anyway." Elliott was looking worriedly at Nazor.

Nazor cocked her head, considering, her dark eyes soft and umber lips pursed. "Why don't we just wait and see what happens? We'll know if she's your cantor soon enough," she intoned. "The Tramors only come to market twice a year, and I'm desperate to get my hands on some Tramorian steel. Besides, I'll only be gone a few weeks."

The slight smile on Nazor's face told Danny that she'd seen all too clearly his discomfort and was purposely steering the conversation toward other topics. He shot her a grateful look, agreed, and returned to his breakfast, his mind full of far more questions than answers.

Elliott seemed not to notice, though, and nodded, clearly persuaded by her reasoning.

Nazor turned to Danny. "As for you, I expect you'll stay fresh on your sword work while I'm gone and take the horses out as often as possible. I don't need either you or them going soft in my absence." Nazor gave Danny a severe look, which he returned with an impish grin.

"Now when've I eva' let you down like that, Nazor?" Danny slipped into his thickest Boston Irish accent, knowing it annoyed her to no end. "I should rightly be offended, on account of I neva' did do nothing to deserve such distrust."

Nazor rolled her eyes and threw her balled up napkin at him. He dodged it, laughing.

"Fair enough," she conceded, trying and failing to hide the small smile that tugged at the corner of her lips. "Care for some quick drill before I go?"

Danny agreed, and they headed outside to the practice field, leaving Elliott smiling and shaking his head as he tidied up the breakfast dishes.

OVER THE NEXT FEW DAYS, Danny tried desperately to put thoughts of the dream and the girl out of his mind. He kept up with his chores and training as Nazor had asked, but even the busy days and aching muscles failed to distract him fully from thoughts of *her*. He'd obviously never met this girl, but strangely felt like he knew her. Elliott seemed to sense his distraction and offered to extend their lessons in Nazor's absence. Danny appreciated this. The mental exhaustion of studying history and languages, not to mention wielding that pulsing energy called pneuma, left him little time for other thoughts.

One afternoon, about a week after Nazor left for Port Galaén, Elliott sent Danny upriver to hunt for a particular herb he was experimenting with as a sleep aid. Danny readily agreed, relieved to have an excuse to get out of the house. He and Elliott had been working on binds, pneumonancy in which the wielder had to use his pneuma to worm his way into other objects and manipulate their structure. Danny was a grounder, so his pneuma was uniquely tied to his person, and he could most adeptly use it to root himself to his surroundings. Canting, or casting your pneuma out, was the opposite of this. It tended to result in a distinct feeling of dissociating from one's body that Danny found disconcerting at best and nauseating at worst. So he couldn't be happier to stretch his legs outside for a bit.

Walking along the water's edge, he felt immediately at ease. Marveling at the fresh smell of grass in the late spring day, he smiled as he turned his face up to absorb the sun's warmth, the sound of flowing water soothing his mind.

He was ripped suddenly back to reality by the snapping of branches and a loud crash as something stumbled out of the forest to his left. His eyes snapped open as his hands grasped automatically for the sword at his hip. Shielding his eyes against the sun, he spun to face the threat.

It was her.

Dark blue eyes blinked at him in confusion, their sapphire depths betraying fear and mistrust above the high cheekbones of her long, oval face. Her thick, unruly curls were dark as espresso beans, and many had escaped the confines of the hair tie meant to fasten them. They spiraled around her face, and Danny was struck with the absurd urge to brush them back behind her ears. Embarrassed by his own foolishness, he sheathed his blade and slowly stepped toward her. He saw her eyes widen, and she swayed dangerously to the side. He put up his hands in what he hoped was a calming gesture as he murmured in a low voice, "It's all right. You're all right. Everything will be fine."

He saw incomprehension in her eyes and stepped toward her reflexively as her knees buckled and she crumpled into a heap. His stomach clenched and he ran toward her, dropping to his knees at her side.

Her eyes were closed, but he was relieved to see her breathing steadily, if somewhat shallowly. Placing an arm on her shoulder, he gave her a gentle shake, but he couldn't rouse her.

"Think, Danny, think," he murmured, feeling a rising sense of panic as he stared at her pale skin. *Was that normal?* He shook his head.

Elliott, he finally decided. *I'll take her to Elliott. He'll know what to do.* Without another thought, Danny scooped her up and half-ran back to the house.

〜

ELLIOTT WAS SHOCKED to see them, and swiftly ushered him in. He helped Danny lay her on a cot in the kitchen as Danny explained how he'd found her. Her eyelids fluttered briefly but remained closed as Elliott bustled back and forth, gathering and chopping herbs he brewed into a tea and assembled as a poultice to place near her head on the cot.

It was only now, with the girl inside and safely under Elliott's watchful care, that Danny let himself feel the rising excitement he'd been too nervous to acknowledge before.

She was alive!

Even after that terrible car accident, here she was, breathing and seemingly unhurt, aside from a few scrapes and bruises. It really was incredible. And after all this time, he would *finally* have his cantor. Danny struggled to get a grip on his excitement.

Hold it together, boy-o, he told himself sternly. *You feel like you know her, but she's got no clue who you are, where she is, or even half the craziness that's headed her way.*

Danny knew, logically, that the surest way to send her running for the hills was to let on that he'd been having creepy stalker dreams about her. He paused his mental castigation at the sight of her stirring, seemingly the poultice at work. Stepping forward, he paused awkwardly, wondering if he should go to her or hang back. The question was solved for him when Elliott swooped down to kneel beside her, his amber eyes kind.

"How are you feeling?" he asked her gently.

THREE

Keira was floating, limbs light and with no telling up from down.

Am I dead?

No, she decided, her head hurt way too much for that.

Slowly, she noticed a cool, damp compress against her forehead. Eyes fluttering, she forced them open a sliver to find wide amber eyes staring down at her, a look of concern clouding their turbulent surface.

"How are you feeling?"

Keira blinked, barely comprehending the question. She sat up, then thought better of it as the room spun. Gingerly, she lay back down, clamping her eyes shut against the swiftly tilting room and wishing for all the world that she had some Dramamine right about then. Hushed murmuring brought her back to the present.

"—to be expected, honestly. It's quite the shock to the system."

"—stumbling out of the forest by the river . . . looked something awful."

The first speaker sounded British, she decided, clinging to the one piece of information she can be sure of. Yes, he had the posh-sounding accent of a BBC reporter. Listening more carefully, she thought the second one was American, but there was a soft lilt to his voice that reminded her of rolling hills. He pronounced the words "rivaa" and "aawful" with the elongated vowels of the East Coast. Maybe Boston?

She groaned aloud. Her muddled brain clearly resented the burden of thought and was rebelling with nauseating vertigo.

After deciding that she was *not* in fact going to vomit, Keira committed resolutely to reopening her eyes, just a sliver. She could certainly manage that.

Yes, she could see now that the British speaker was the same amber-eyed man with the damp cloth as before. Keira paused for a moment and, sensing no impending vertigo, opened her eyes wider. He seemed a slightly older man, not yet middle-aged but with lines already creasing his eyes and mouth. His long, russet auburn hair was streaked with gold above a high forehead.

The other was the man she'd seen at the river—younger, maybe early twenties, with sandy blond hair that flopped into his eyes as he spoke. While she was watching them, he turned light olive-green eyes in her direction, and a wide, toothy grin lit up his face, making her want to smile back despite herself. Seeing the younger man's diverted attention, Amber Eyes turned toward her.

"Oh, well done! Tell me, how *are* you feeling?" He strode toward her and, picking up a steaming cup from the bench beside her, offered it for her to sip. "Careful now, it's quite hot."

Warily, Keira eased herself into a sitting position, eyeing them both as she grasped the proffered mug. Warm, not-too-sweet tea slid down her suddenly parched throat. Remembering the man's warning, she had to stop herself from gulping the steaming liquid as she realized just how thirsty she was. While she drank, the man watched her with a level of interest one usually reserved for strange and exotic creatures. Keira shifted, eyes darting between the two of them, and the younger man cleared his throat pointedly.

"So sorry, how rude of me." The older man exclaimed, laughing. "My name is Elliott. Danny here is the one who found you stumbling out of the woods by the river fork, looking quite the worse for wear, I must say. He brought you here, hoping I might be of some use. I have a penchant for the healing craft," he confessed. "And you, what's your name?"

His voice had a forced nonchalance to it but Keira could practically see his eagerness in the rapid drumming of his fingers against his side. She cleared her throat, buying herself a moment before croaking, "Keira." She swallowed, trying to clear it further before adding, "Keira Altman."

Until this point, Keira had paid little mind to her surroundings. But as she swept a wary eye around the room's interior, she was surprised to see something like a hunting lodge, complete with burning fire and wooden furniture—which evidently explained the creaky cot she found herself on now. More to the point, peering at the pair of men in front of her, she realized with a start that they were decked out in clothes that most closely resembled the standard garb of your average Renaissance fair. The older man, Elliott, wore a long, sage-green robe made of rough-looking fabric and belted at the waist. The younger one, Danny, wore a loose cloth tunic belted over leather pants. Looking back to Elliott, who'd apparently been explaining something about the tea, she interrupted, "Sorry, are you both re-enactors or something?" Her confusion deepened as Keira caught the wary glance that flashed between the two.

"Not exactly . . ." Elliott replied. "Keira, do you, by chance, remember what the date was when you left?"

"Left?" Keira stared at him, uncomprehending. Then the memories began pouring in. She sat bolt upright. "The car!" Turning to Elliott, who looked curious but calm despite her outburst, she begged, "Please, help me find the car! My mom and I were driving. It was raining and we started spinning out. I don't remember what happened, but when I woke up, I couldn't find them."

She was pleading at this point, and her eyes stung. "It's my mom and Molly, about seven years old. Sh-she's got blonde pigtails, and her dress is pink, or blue, or something. Please, they need our *help*." Keira moved to get off the cot, but firm hands eased her back down. Confused, Keira said, "Please, she's just a little girl. She needs help, and my mom, well, she'll be looking for m—"

"Keira," Elliott interrupted, giving her a long, piercing look. "They're not here."

"What? No, I mean, they can't be far. I must have been thrown from the car when—"

"Keira," Elliott said again. "This will be very hard to understand, but the place that you have come from, it is very far away and very different from where you are now. In fact, you could say that it's another world entirely."

Keira searched around desperately, trying to think of how to communicate the urgency of finding the car. Seeing her lack of attention, Elliott tried a different tack.

"Keira, where and when do you think you are?"

Keira stared at him, wondering if she'd heard the question correctly. Seeing that she had, and that he meant it earnestly, she replied slowly, "I don't know, just off the five north?" Seeing his confused look, she clarified, "Northern California."

Elliott nodded, as if this made sense.

"And the date?"

"May second."

Seeing his expectant look, she said slowly, as if to a small child, "2017." Elliott smiled widely, and behind him, she saw Danny's eyes widen.

"That is where you have come from," Elliott said. "Where you are is a country called Loren in the year 236 of the Marian Era, in a world very different from the one you know."

Keira opened and shut her mouth, trying to think of how to reply. This had to be a joke, but neither man seemed to find it particularly funny. Keira could hear Elliott continuing to explain something, but she was having a hard time focusing and caught only snippets as her head swam again.

". . . between worlds is uncommon, but possible . . . particular ability lets you cast your essence. . . called pneuma—"

Keira had had enough of this. Shoving off the blanket, she swung her legs off of the cot and stood up, brushing off helpful hands in irritation. Turning on both sets of curious eyes, she said, "I'm leaving now." The stern set of her mouth dared either of them to contradict her. Neither did. "Where is the nearest town?" she demanded.

After a brief pause, the one named Danny spoke up. He had been silent until this point, but now said, "Just south. You can follow the path that runs along the river."

"Thanks," she snapped, her irritation making her tone harsher than intended. She turned back to Elliott.

"I appreciate the tea, but it's time I was going." She strode out the door, and neither of them tried to stop her.

FOUR

Danny watched the door slam shut behind Keira, leaving a confusing mess of emotions in her wake.

When she'd first arrived, Danny had been too nervous to join Elliott at the table—pacing the room while his mentor explained that this was largely to be expected when one's pneuma crossed worlds. The body it entered was an exact copy of the one it had left, but it still took some time to adjust. Sure enough, she'd been in and out for the first few minutes, but eventually she was sitting up and drinking the tea that Elliott had prepared, color slowly coming back into her skin.

Thinking back, Danny remembered waking up in Loren with a splitting headache and puking his guts out. He thought this girl seemed to be doing better—at least physically. Mentally, she seemed more than a little terrified by the whole situation. When she'd said she was from the year 2017, he'd felt his mouth fall open. He quickly shut it but struggled even harder not to stare at her, taking in the blue jeans and long-sleeved shirt she wore with a hood on the back. He was seventy years older than her! And he'd thought they'd have so much in common. Who knew how much had changed between his time and hers?

He'd only been in Loren for a little over a year. Could time really move so differently between the two worlds? Danny decided that this was a thought for another day and turned his attention back to Elliott and an increasingly agitated Keira. Elliott was trying to explain all about pneuma and the Legion, the organization that Elliott and Nazor served. In typical Elliott fashion, he was providing way more information than she could possibly process in the present moment.

Give her a minute, Danny thought with futility. *She's only just arrived.* Of course, Elliott couldn't hear him, and Keira's emphatic head shakes became fiercer, until clearly, she'd finally had enough. When she demanded to know where the nearest town was, Danny decided it was best she saw for herself and gave her the directions.

She thanked him and promptly strode out the door without a second look back, clearly fed up with their antics. Elliott turned to Danny with a sheepish look. "I guess I might have gotten a bit carried away."

Danny gave him a sardonic smile.

"You think?"

He said nothing further though as he stared after her, fighting the warring emotions of concern and . . . disappointment. Was this really the cantor he'd waited so long for? His partner across time and worlds? The girl could barely look at him and seemed weak as a lamb. Though the thought pricked him with guilt, he couldn't help but wonder if there'd had been some sort of mistake.

As if reading his mind, Elliott laid a hand gently on his shoulder.

"Give her time, Danny. Everything happens for a reason, you know that."

Danny tried for a smile but knew the expression came out more stricken than anything.

"It's alright to be disappointed, Danny. But try to remember this is all very new to her. She just needs *time*."

Well, now he really did feel like a cad.

"Of course. I know that, I—I just . . ." Danny searched for words that didn't come and he shrugged helplessly. "You're right. She just needs time."

Elliott smiled knowingly before clapping his hands on the table and springing back into motion. He quickly busied himself stripping the cot.

"You'll follow her, then?" He asked around the gathered pile of blankets. "If she feels overwhelmed now, it'll only be worse when she sees Abalás."

Danny nodded and bent to grab his cloak.

"I'd keep your distance at first, though. Wait until it all becomes a bit too much and then let her know she has a place here if she'd like it." Elliott shrugged. "That's really all we can do."

Danny inhaled the last dregs of a summer breeze as he surveyed the sky, listening as the heavy door slammed shut behind him. Before long, fall would be there in full and the leaves would begin their slow, inexorable change. Keira wouldn't survive a winter here on her own. He saw that clearly. He just had to make sure she did as well.

~

KEIRA MOVED QUICKLY, as if she might outrun the strangeness of the whole situation. She didn't know who those people were or where they got off scaring the crap out of car crash victims, but she'd had enough. There just wasn't time. Her mother and Molly needed her and she needed to get help—real help. Her fingers tapped rhythmically against her leg, as if they might chase away the fear curdling in her stomach. She'd let herself feel that later, but not now.

She found the path Danny had mentioned easily enough and, keeping the river on her left, had been following it for half an hour when she saw smoke in the distance. Hurrying now, she rounded a bend in the path and stopped dead in her tracks.

In front of her, the path merged with a wide road that came out of the forest to her right and met with a great stone bridge that spanned the length of the river she'd been following. This road was clearly well-traveled, as people bustled over the bridge and about their business, all dressed in rough homespun dresses and tunics that looked practically medieval. Many were laughing as they greeted those coming from the opposite direction, leading horses and oxen bearing wagons laden with baskets of food, bundles of hay, and other items fit for a farmer's market.

A shout brought Keira's attention to the river she'd been following, as ahead of her men floated downstream, riding rafts of great tree trunks lashed together. The men called to the people on the bridge as they floated their cargo underneath toward the town that lay beyond. The town, Keira now saw, was filled with one- and two-story houses made of white plastered timber.

Her mouth had gone completely dry and her legs felt numb as her mind struggled to take in the reality her eyes insisted to be true.

No. This is not happening. It can't be.

Keira shook her head vigorously, as if she might clear the sight from her mind's eye by sheer force of will. *There has to be some sort of explanation*, her always rational brain insisted. *You just have to find it.*

Buoyed by this conviction that had never steered her wrong, Keira took a deep breath and strode forward, determined to find someone who could help her, or at least explain what the hell was going on.

Holding her head stiffly erect, Keira strode across the bridge, trying her very best to ignore the looks of shock and bewilderment people gave her. Suddenly feeling very conscious of the tattered jeans and sweatshirt that she wore, she tried to avoid eye contact as she hurried into town. Surely there had to be a visitor's center or tourism office, right?

When she made it into town, the sights and *smells* of a market immediately accosted her senses. Fish mongers hawked their wares as they shooed sniffing dogs away from their product. Farmers at their stalls proudly displayed their baskets and crates of fresh, sweet-smelling produce. The large, open square was filled to the brim with people buying and selling, laughing, and catching up on the week's gossip. Keira spun around, feeling the people and noise crushing in on her from all sides, as she fought hard against the rising sense of panic. There was no one else dressed in normal clothes, and when she asked a helpful-looking and very pregnant woman dressed as a fishwife if she could point her toward the visitor center, the woman looked at her like she was a raving lunatic.

"Visitin' are ye? Well, that explains loads." She eyed Keira up and down. "Hob-nogged downlanders," she muttered to herself. "Ye'll be wantin' the tavern over there." She pointed across the square and waddled away.

There was that panic again. Nobody spoke like that in Northern California. Keira just focused on breathing.

In through her nose. Out through her mouth.

Feeling the sudden urge to escape, Keira hurried towards the tavern but couldn't help but stop to gawk at two passing columns of men in blood red robes, their low-voiced chants emanating from unseen faces beneath bowed and hooded heads. She gave them a wide berth before heading inside, where her questions about police and phones were met with blank looks and wary expressions. These folks clearly were not exactly used to visitors, especially strange ones who walked around in ripped jeans. Desperate, Keira went back outside and held her now-throbbing head in her hands. She tried to slow her breathing, which was now coming hard and fast. She willed her heart rate to slow, to stop the painful pulsing in her ears.

None of this was helping.

She had to *think*. She had to *understand*. But the harder she tried, the more the pieces just would not come together. None of this made sense and Keira leaned forward, clutching tightly at the edge of the wooden step as the edges of her vision darkened. Was this a panic attack? That distant medical part of her wondered. She'd never had one before, but this matched all the descriptions. Unfortunately, nothing was coming to mind about what to actually do about it...

A warm hand on her shoulder slowly brought her back to reality. Keira glanced up to see kind green eyes as Danny kneeled beside her.

"Just breathe," he said quietly. "You're here. You're alive. Everything is going to be alright."

Keira felt herself nodding as she squeezed her eyes shut, forcing her breathing to slow, matching his, breath for breath. Slowly, the thrumming of her pulse in her ears slowed and she blinked up at him. Danny smiled gently and offered her a hand. Roughly shoving aside tears, she took it and he pulled her to her feet.

"You feel steady?" He asked, and she nodded because, surprisingly, she did.

"Then come with me."

Not exactly having a better idea, Keira followed him. Danny led her past an ornate circular building at the top of the town square and through a door at the base of a bell tower to its side. They ascended narrow spiral stairs for what seemed an eternity until they emerged through a trapdoor at the top and into a tiny room made all the smaller by the massive bells that filled it nearly to capacity. Keira followed Danny over to one of the great windows to the side and slowly approached it, acutely concerned that her fear of heights might stoke the all-too-fresh bouts of nausea she'd been wrestling with earlier.

But as she approached, she recognized what Danny had wanted her to see. High above the trees as they were, Keira could see not only the market and town below them but also the massive lake, whose banks the town sat upon. Beyond this, Keira could see vast expanses of land sloping down from them, and far off in the distance, a wedge of sea that she could just make out sliced inland as arable lands swelled around its intrusion.

"That," Danny said, gesturing at the lake, "is Lake Abel. The town we're in now is called Abalás. Over there," he said, motioning to the wedge of sea, "is the Fertile Inlet. A river runs from Lake Abel all the way to Port Galaén. The river plains nourish all the farms in that area as water drains into the inlet."

Keira stared out at what he'd described, trying desperately to make sense of it.

"You are not in California anymore," Danny told her softly, and she knew in that moment that he was right.

"Also, I think this belongs to you," Danny held out his hand and in his palm lay her mother's gold locket, its chain still broken. Keira swallowed a choked sob as she gingerly took it from him.

"You dropped it as I brought you into the cabin. I would have given it to you before, but . . ." Danny rubbed a hand across the back of his neck, looking sheepish.

"I was too busy freaking out?" Keira asked, forcing out a quivering laugh as she pressed the metal into her palm.

Danny shrugged. "You had your reasons."

She felt tears fill her eyes again, marveling at his quiet kindness, and she roughly squeezed her fists against them, groaning.

"I promise I don't normally cry this much," she said.

His hand brushed her arm and he offered her a small smile as she looked up at him.

"It's a lot. I get it. I tell you, I was the same, if not worse."

She stared at him, surprised. "Really? You're like me? I-I mean, not from here?"

His smile widened and his eyes softened, considering her almost shyly.

"More than you know."

CHAPTER

FIVE

Keira awoke to light filtering in through the latched shutters above the tiny bed in the attic room she'd retreated to the night before. As the dawning reality of wakefulness flooded her senses, so too did the disappointment that accompanied her attic surroundings. She was not, in fact, safely tucked away in her new dorm room at Stanford, but in an unfamiliar attic in a very strange new world.

In the light of day, she could see that it was sparsely decorated, the wood cot and a rickety chair the only furniture aside from a small chest of drawers. Yet the fresh flowers and filled water pitcher on top of the chest told her that someone had done their best to bring some homey touches to the room. The thick, hand-sewn quilt of rich red and blue fabric that she was currently curled up under confirmed this suspicion.

She thought back to the day before, when Danny had convinced her to return with him to the small cottage. She'd agreed because frankly it was her only option—the idea of sleeping outside in the elements, a decidedly unappealing one. But she had no intention of staying. If she made it here, she could make it back. The quietly intense Danny and eccentric Elliott must know a way, if only she could pry it out of them. And one way or another, she was determined to find her way home—back to her life, back to her mom.

Her fingers tightened absently over the smooth lettering on the broken locket—the last gift her mother ever gave her. God knew her mom wasn't perfect, but they had always had each other, no matter what.

"I'll find a way, Mom. I promise you that."

She would have liked to have stayed tucked away forever, had it not been for the rumbling she heard coming from her stomach.

Reluctantly, she slid out from underneath her warm covers and stepped gingerly onto the rough-hewn floorboards. Chilly as it was, she wrapped the old quilt around her shoulders and plodded toward the door, feeling comforted and oddly protected by its substantial weight.

Stepping out into the hallway, she heard a faint, lyrical humming coming from below, and the unmistakable smell of freshly fried bacon wafted up to her. Her stomach growled again to remind her of its deprivation and otherwise ill-treatment the day before. Conceding, she carefully eased her way down the tightly twisting staircase to the warm kitchen below. Elliott stood at a worktable against the far window, scraping freshly cut herbs into a stone mortar and grinding them into a thick paste with a pestle.

"I've left you some fresh bacon on the stove and buttered bread underneath that cloth over there." Elliott gestured over his shoulder with his pestle. "Danny's out working with the horses, but he'll be back in for lunch around midday."

"Oh, umm . . . thanks."

Keira eyed Elliott warily before shuffling over to what must have been the stovetop, oddly shaped though it was. It looked to be made of an ironlike material of some sort. She scooped a few pieces of bacon onto the plate Elliott had left out for her. It smelled heavenly, and she quickly bit into the largest piece, her eyes closing in rapture. She heard chuckling and opened one eye to see Elliott smiling at her. She shrugged at him. "I've never been one to turn down free food."

"Sensible girl."

"So, what's with the stove?" Keira asked between eager bites. "Isn't this supposed to be the Dark Ages or something? At the Renaissance fair, everybody had to cook over open fires." Even just saying it made Keira feel ridiculous. Elliott didn't laugh though, continuing to grind his herbs as he added small dribbles of water from a nearby tankard until it reached a paste-like consistency.

"An open fire is far more common here, yes," Elliott explained in that thick BBC accent of his. "One advantage of coming from other times and places is that it gives you superb ideas on how to reduce the soot content of the average kitchen." Elliott eyed her over his shoulder. "We also bathe more than your average villager, placing a higher premium on clean clothes and personal hygiene." Keira blushed at this, remembering that she was still wearing the same clothes from yesterday, though she doubted Elliott had meant his comments to be pointed.

"But remember," Elliott continued, sounding professorial, "this isn't the actual Dark Ages, at least not so far as you learned about them. Well, first of all, it could be argued that it far more closely resembles classical antiquity." He actually sounded excited now. "But we are actually in an entirely different world, with different lands and where ideas and innovations travel differently. For instance, we've managed to configure a pump outside that draws from our well. It's all really quite exciting!" Keira couldn't help but smile at his obvious delight and tried in vain to stifle the yawn that came suddenly, unbidden.

Elliott cocked his head, looking sheepish. "You must still be exhausted. I've laid out some clean clothes for you by the washtub in the back room." He smiled kindly.

Ok, Keira thought, *maybe his earlier comment* was *pointed*. Regardless, Keira thanked him and went outside to draw up the water she'd need for her bath. The filling bucket was not very large, and it took Keira several trips to manage it. She'd all but resigned herself to the cold dunking that awaited her hard work and was about to pull off her sweatshirt when Elliott knocked on the door to the back room. She opened it for him.

"Just a moment," Elliott said.

Kneeling by the filled washtub, he reached a long white hand into the water, letting the water flow through his fingers. He closed his eyes and hummed a single long note to himself. Keira was just about to ask what exactly he was trying to do when she noticed gentle ripples begin under the surface. Keira could only stare as the ripples turned to bubbles, which themselves popped on the surface and emitted a gentle steam into the air. When he was clearly satisfied with his work, Elliott withdrew his hand, wiping it on his tunic as he stood up. Keira could only gape at him as he grinned widely, clearly proud of himself.

"*Now* it's ready."

"H-How? W-What on earth did you do?" Keira stammered, barely coherent.

Elliott just smiled before pointing and sternly replying, "First, bathe. Then we'll talk."

He strode out of the room, leaving Keira staring at her now near-scalding bathwater and wondering just what she had gotten herself into.

∼

As Keira stretched languidly in the steaming bath, she could feel her muscles slowly unwind, bringing solace that not even sleep could offer. At that moment, she could have been anywhere, in a spa somewhere, or even just back at her apartment off campus. She inhaled the steaming vapor through flared nostrils and opened her eyes. The wood-paneled back room of the small farmhouse greeted her with its muted tones of earthy beige. She sighed.

She still couldn't wrap her mind around everything that had happened. Somehow, impossibly, she had left the only world she'd ever known. But how was that possible? She was a scientist, after all, or trying to be. She was destined for medical school and life as a physician. Was she prepared to accept this new and unexplained reality into her cosmic worldview? She shook her head.

But I saw it.

She'd watched Elliott heat the water with his bare hands. No one could create heat from nothing; that much she knew undeniably. Then how did he do it? She was itching to ask him, to make him explain it to her, but something in her resisted, unwilling to be suckered into whatever trick this must be. She refused to believe she was really alone. Her mom had to be out there somewhere.

Sure, Keira and her mom, Tammy, had never had the most normal of mother-daughter relationships. Keira's dad had taken off before she'd even started walking. Tammy had done her best; Keira had to give her that. But being a young, single mom was a tough gig under the best of circumstances, and Lord knew Tammy's circumstances were never the best. Keira had never met her grandparents, but had certainly heard stories. Between her flighty mother and alcoholic father, Tammy had spent her childhood dreaming of escape. When she finally did, she set about to make a better life for herself than the one she'd grown up with. And as Norman Rockwell and the Hallmark channel had made evidently clear, a better life required a man.

Keira didn't know much about her father. Tammy had alternately flat out refused to talk about him or else spun the most obviously absurd fairy tales, which Keira couldn't help but laugh at, quickly defusing that line of inquiry. The only thing Keira knew for certain was that he had existed and that somewhere along the line, he'd left.

Deeply insecure, Tammy had spent the years that followed flitting between men, exchanging one loser for another until they became a spinning carousel in Keira's memory, one painted ass indistinguishable from the next.

Keira glanced down to realize that her hands had balled into fists, her nails biting into her wrinkled palms. With a deep breath, she willed herself to unfold them. Her relationship with her mother was . . . complicated, to say the least. A pang of guilt cut through her. What if her mom was out there somewhere, looking for her? Keira wasn't sure how this whole cross-worlds thing worked. Did time move differently here?

Then an even worse possibility sprung to mind—what if she wasn't the only one killed in that car accident?

Keira quickly shoved the thought from her mind. Her mom was the only family she'd ever had. Even the knowledge that Keira may never see her again was better than the possibility that she may have simply ceased to exist.

Besides, there had to be a way back. If people could cross worlds, surely they could cross back. She pressed her fingertips briefly into her temples before resolutely heaving herself out of the tub. One way or another, she would figure out what the hell was going on.

CHAPTER

SIX

Combing out her damp curls with her fingers, Keira came into the kitchen to find Elliott still at work on his mysterious paste concoction. Looking up, he gestured to an open chair, and Keira complied, uneasily shifting about in the belted tunic and drawstring pants Elliott had laid out, both a rusty shade that reminded Keira unsettlingly of blood. Keira shivered, remembering the events of the day before, or whenever it was. To distract herself, she launched into her pre-rehearsed line of inquiry.

"So, that, uh, water thing. That's what you were talking about yesterday, your pneuma . . . whatever it was you called it."

It wasn't really a question, but Elliott replied as if it were.

"Yes, pneumonancy. That's part of it, yes."

Elliott paused then to rinse his hands in the washbasin to his left before joining Keira at the table. Toweling his hands dry, he fixed Keira with a direct amber stare. Behind the frank kindness, Keira sensed a calculating mind, weighing and measuring exactly how much to tell her—how much she could take.

"The word comes from the Greek *pneuma*, meaning 'air,' or in this case, more accurately translated as 'spirit.'"

"My Greeks or your Greeks?" Keira joked weakly, shifting uncomfortably as she imagined what else Elliott might boil with this strange air gift of his.

Elliott just smiled and continued, "We're called pneumonancers, or 'spirit-binders', according to local legend. We're known for our ability to use pneuma to manipulate things around us, objects, animals . . . even people." Elliott paused, peering at Keira cautiously. "What is it you did in your world? Did you work, study?"

Keira blinked, startled by the change in subject.

"I'm about to start college. I hope to be a doctor someday. If—" Keira halted, rubbing her nose to fight the sting that usually signaled imminent tears.

"I mean 'was.' I *was* about to start college," she amended, staring at the flower arrangement on the table to avoid meeting Elliott's sympathetic gaze.

He was smiling and nodding, as if something had confirmed his suspicions. "Then you've studied how the universe works, what you call 'science' but has gone by many names through the ages. Now, I told you that things work differently here, which is true. But there are some things that hold steady across worlds, and pneuma is one of those things. You've learned about sound waves, yes?" Elliott glanced at Keira, searching for comprehension. Keira nodded slowly, not seeing how sound waves applied to some magical Jedi spirit-force.

"I'm sure you learned how sound waves are patterns of disturbance caused by the movement of energy through a medium such as air."

Keira continued to nod, wondering where on earth all this was going.

"That is . . . more or less . . . how pneuma works. It is like an energy, unique to every person and that specially trained individuals have some control over. It is a powerful force with the ability to disrupt the natural arrangement of what you would call molecules and atoms. Although, in reality, 'natural' is such an inaccurate term to use, as who's to say what the progenitor of true order really is . . ." Elliott trailed off and laughed quietly, shaking his head at the look of confusion and mounting discomfort on Keira's face.

"But I digress. Apologies, I can get a little carried away on this subject. My point is that pneumonancers like me have learned to manipulate our pneuma, altering the size and shape of the waves it makes as it travels through various mediums. These waves can then add to or subtract from the pneuma that exists in our mark, the target of our pneumonancy, until we can alter its form, causing things like water to boil."

Keira just stared at him.

"So . . . " she began, finally regaining her wits. "Can you see this pneuma stuff?"

Keira imagined the sparking wands and wizarding duels she'd seen in movies growing up.

Elliott merely shook his head. "Pneuma itself cannot be seen, only its effects. It can, however, with the proper training, be heard," he explained. "Just as we can detect sound waves using the specialized organs we call ears, pneumonancers can learn to not only detect pneuma but distinguish it by type and origin, a powerful skill." Elliott nodded gravely, then gave Keira a considering look. "And one I hope you'll let me teach you one day."

Keira's face shot up from its seat in her hands, where she'd been meticulously kneading her temples as she tried to process all of this. The scientist in her relished this new and fascinating discovery and the idea of learning more about pneuma and the strange Legion of pneumonancers that Elliott had mentioned the night before. There was another part of her, though, that still felt raw. So much had changed and so suddenly that it was threatening to overwhelm her.

"I still don't understand what the purpose is in all of this," Keira moaned, lashing out rather than accept feeling so tiny in the face of these things she just couldn't understand. "I die, and you're somehow able to yank me out of my world and into this one. You still haven't explained that one yet, by the way. And for what? To learn some magic tricks? It doesn't make sense."

Keira's blurring eyes had overflowed by now, and her nose continued to burn with her efforts to control her growing feeling of desperation. "I'm dead and everything and everyone I've ever cared about is over, done, never to be seen or experienced by me again, and I'm supposed to . . . what? Be comforted that I'll get to learn how to play with magic? That's my life now? I need some friggin' answers, because right now this all feels like the worst cosmic joke imaginable."

Elliott didn't answer right away. His gaze merely held hers, as if he was weighing how best to respond. Long moments later, he finally continued. "I don't blame you for being confused. I was far older than you when I first made the journey, and that was many lifetimes ago. I was a graduate student at Oxford back in your world. Did I tell you that?"

Keira shook her head.

"I loved that life, as I'm sure you loved yours. I studied and taught physics, and I loved my work. It gave me meaning and purpose, helped me understand the world around me. But sometimes things happen to us that we can never fully understand. It took me an extraordinarily long time to understand what the Legion could possibly have in mind for—"

"The Legion?" Keira interjected. "What's the Legion?"

Elliott froze, eyes widening in a surprisingly accurate imitation of a rabbit caught in the crosshairs.

"Well," he began, rubbing the back of his neck and looking decidedly uncomfortable. "The Legion was . . . *is* . . . an organization. One that transcends worlds. In order to understand them, one must first understand . . . Oh, how to explain it? Well, it's just tha—" A thought seemed suddenly to occur to him then, and he spun to face her, eyes gleaming. "Do you know what entropy is?"

Keira stared at him, trying to suppress the growing frustration at this obvious evasion of her question. She succeeded enough to spit out a response. "The measure of disorder in a system."

"Exactly. You see, everything in the universe trends toward greater and greater disorder. Because of entropy, we have an explanation for why the universe is always expanding, leaving a void that must be filled. Yet even as more and more worlds are created to fill this void, the creation of this order out of chaos releases energy that further fuels the universe's expansion and disorder. My *point*," he emphasized, seeing Keira about to interrupt angrily, "in saying all this is that things naturally fall apart, energy and matter delocalize, and order breaks down."

He paused, catching Keira's glare.

"Our purpose, that is, the Legion's purpose, is to fight against entropy itself, to create order out of the chaos and prevent, or at the very least, slow down, the gradual march of the universe toward chaos. In broad strokes, that is what we do: we restore order when things fall apart. As for what our purpose is in this world at this very moment—the hinge point that has called you and Danny to this time and place—well, that is a conversation for another day."

Keira shook her head, still not quite believing that this was happening. Could all this really be true? She had to admit she had no better explanation for how she'd ended up in this place, surrounded by people dressed like medieval re-enactors who boiled water with their bare hands. It was enough to make even the most hardened skeptic, as Keira used to think of herself, take pause and consider the possibility that the universe was far larger and more complex than the simple models and laws in her textbooks could articulate. Keira honestly didn't know what to make of all of this, and so she focused on the smallest piece she could think of to puzzle out.

"So when you made the water boil . . . you were creating disorder, right? Changing it from a liquid to a gas."

Elliott beamed at her. "Very good! It's one of the easier things to do, as matter only needs a little nudge to proceed in the direction it's inclined to go toward, anyway."

Elliott's smile twisted a bit at this, and Keira had the distinct impression that they weren't just discussing water anymore. "Anyone can break things apart," he explained ruefully. "The true test is whether you can put them back together again. Destroying is sometimes necessary. It is, after all, required for eating, defending oneself, and breaking down the materials needed to one day build up. The Legion's founding mandate is that its members create more order than they do disorder, build more than they break."

"That seems rather bleak," Keira muttered, and Elliott smiled at her ruefully.

"Yes, yes it does, I suppose. But against all odds, the Legion persists. In this country, they're based out of Port Galaén, and there they've built their great library, filled to the brim with all we know and have yet to unravel about the functioning of Pneumos. You'll see it when you attend the rites. That is . . . if you choose to join us, that is."

Keira's gaze shot up, interest piqued.

"Does it—" she hesitated. "Would it explain about how we cross worlds?"

Elliott hesitated, eyeing Keira cautiously.

"Yes, all the answers we seek can be found there, but it often takes many lifetimes to master its secrets. The library can be . . . finicky."

Keira swallowed. *Lifetimes?*

But gritting her teeth, she slowly nodded. If lifetimes were what it took to find a way back to her world, her life, her mom, then she would prove herself to this Legion and gain access to its knowledge . . . no matter how long it took.

"And it's your Greeks."

Startled, Keira refocused on the present moment. "What?"

"Your earlier question. The word *pneuma* comes from your Greeks, the only Greeks. Remember, it's not that you went back in time; you've come to a wholly different world, one that functions very differently than the one you're used to. We call this world we're in now Carnos, and the particular country we're in is called Loren. Carnos has its own history, varied cultures, and unique problems that did not exist where you come from. I know it's a lot," he said, seeing Keira's panicked expression. "But it will come to feel normal. I promise."

Not sure exactly what to say, Keira asked the first question that came to mind. "What's my world called?"

"Primos," Elliott replied, a doleful look on his face. "It is the first world, the one that started it all. A little cosmos-centric, I'll grant you, but it's the world all Legionnaires came from at one point or another." Keira thought about this, not fully convinced. But then again, what could convincingly explain all that she'd seen and experienced?

She shook her head ruefully but then stopped as a thought suddenly occurred to her.

"When did you, umm—leave, then? Our world, I mean."

Elliott looked wistful, as if remembering a far-off place or a life half-forgotten. "1877."

Keira stared at him, waiting for a punchline that never came. Then, shaking his head slightly, Elliott turned back to her. "That's enough for now. Come, let's go find Danny, and we'll show you around."

Not sure what else to do, Keira stood and followed him outside.

Elliott inhaled deeply the morning air, a broad smile of utter contentment tugging at his lips. "There's really nothing quite like—"

Elliott's words were drowned out by sudden raucous cries. Elliott's head jerked up and Keira saw him visibly pale. She followed his gaze to see a massive flock of birds emerging from the treetops. But instead of flying with the coordinated unison she was used to, the flight of these birds seemed . . . disjointed. They flew in all directions, barely avoiding collision, their wings flapping with a lopsided stiffness that seemed at odds with the graceful slope of their wings. Keira searched in vain for whatever predator pursued them . . . but there was nothing.

Creepy, Keira thought, shivering despite herself.

"So this library," she started, turning back to Elliott as she tried and failed to keep her voice light. "You mentioned the Legion had one nearby? That it might explain more about this whole world-crossing thing?"

Elliott didn't answer, but continued to stare at the birds—jaw clenched and brow furrowed.

"Elliott?" She asked again, tugging nervously at her tunic as she glanced up once more at the swarming birds, their off-kilter flight growing more off-putting by the second.

"Elliott, what is that?"

Her question finally startled him out of his reverie. He glanced down at her, frown melting in an instant and replaced by an affable grin.

"Oh nothing, starling migration just a bit early this year."

Keira frowned dubiously, her eyes tracking the flock of birds as they vanished over the horizon. She knew he was a scholar, but still . . .

"As for the Legion's library, I'm afraid it's in Port Galaén, quite a distance from here." he continued. "Not a journey to be taken lightly, I'm afraid, especially by one so new to this world. But if it's reading you're looking for, I'd happily offer my own library. It's nothing in comparison, of course, but I am something of a collector and I'm sure you'll find plenty there to entertain yourself."

Keira smiled tightly in return, thanking him, before turning to follow him out to the stable. One thing was certain, she had questions —about chaos, the Legion, and this strange new world she found herself in. And if books held the answers, then she'd find them.

No matter what it took.

CHAPTER
SEVEN

Danny inhaled deeply, relishing the scent of freedom as he made his way, wagon and all, toward Abalás. He needed this, needed to escape the nervous confines of the cottage. The three of them rarely ventured into town, preferring to keep to themselves on the outskirts. All the better to train and ensure the Legion's activities remained secret, Nazor had explained. Still, it could be lonely. Nazor and Elliott had each other, but Danny often wished he could befriend one of the many young men that lived in and around the village.

Just wait until your cantor arrives, Nazor had told him. *You'll have all the company you could want—more even.*

Hey, Elliott had protested. *I'll have you know I make for splendid company.*

This had rapidly descended into flirtatious banter, and Danny had quickly excused himself.

Normally, he didn't mind. He enjoyed spending time with Nazor and Elliott. They were likely older, wiser siblings . But just then, their easy companionship had felt like a kick in the gut. He'd reminded himself that Nazor was right. Soon his cantor would arrive and he'd have a friend, a companion of his own.

So much for that, Danny thought ruefully.

It wasn't that he *disliked* Keira. She was just nothing like what he'd expected. He'd expected his cantor to be like Nazor—strong, stoic, capable. Keira was certainly . . . softer. But she was also wholly different from any of the girls he'd known back home—with their giggling and sidelong glances.

In short, he found her . . . odd. She had a tendency to skulk around the house, eyeing both him and Elliott with wary eyes, as if either was about to sprout horns at any moment. She'd offered to help with chores, but otherwise was content to just watch and *read*.

That might be the oddest thing, Danny decided. In all his, admittedly brief, life, he'd met no one who could read like Keira Altman. He'd be out with the horses, enjoying the cool late summer breeze and she'd stay perched beneath a giant oak tree, completely engrossed for hours and buried nose deep in a book. What's more, it never seemed to be the *same* book. And judging from the rate at which she flipped the pages, she was actually *finishing* them all. Before long, she'd make quick work of even Elliott's impressive collection. Seeing this made Elliott beam with a sort of fatherly pride, but Danny looked on with something more akin to suspicion.

He'd never much understood reading as a pastime, never understood the appeal of dusty tomes and long-winded explanations—not when you could be outside enjoying fresh air and actually *doing* things. To each their own, he supposed, but it cemented in his mind what he'd long suspected — Keira Altman was *not* the cantor he'd been waiting for.

Sure Elliott was a cantor who enjoyed his books, but he also filled his days training and practicing pneumonancy. Keira had yet to show the slightest inclination to do either. Danny had been an Army corporal in his other life, had seen what happened when green and inexperienced kids showed up to fight in wars they had no business going anywhere near.

And war was coming.

He could feel it in the shifting winds, in the murmured conversations and sidelong glances of the townsfolk. Peace was all he'd known since arriving in this world and Pneumos knew he'd needed it, but things were changing and he didn't know how long Keira had to get up to speed on all she needed to know.

Danny shook his head, scowling so ferociously that travelers walking opposite on the road from Abalás gave him a wide, weary berth.

Calm down, he ordered himself, feeling sheepish as a grandmotherly woman gathered a small flock of children close as she scowled right back at him. Elliott had told him to give her time, but it had been several days since she'd arrived and he was growing impatient.

Danny shoved the thoughts roughly from his mind as he reached the western bridge that led into town. He had supplies to purchase and news of the town to gather. The many mysteries of Keira Altman would just have to wait.

Just then, something caught his attention and he reigned Boyd to a halt.

A great grove of oak trees stood along the riverbank. Older than the town itself these oak trees had stood guard over the bridge into town since its construction. Danny must have passed them hundreds of times over the last year. But something now seemed . . . off.

Kneeing Boyd forward, Danny got a better look at the closest Oak and gasped. The trunk's bark was scourged in a diagonal shape, as if burned. Black tendrils twisted up the tree surface leaving whole arms dead and decaying. And from the center of the blackness, a single white fungated mass bloomed to life.

Danny shivered, wondering what strange disease could have blighted these ancient trees so. Regardless, he doubted there was much he could do now. So with one last regretful look back, he urged Boyd into town.

~

Stepping into the general store, Danny found a small group of day laborers engaged in a heated discussion at the counter. So Danny leaned against a nearby counter, pretending to survey its wares as he eavesdropped on their conversation.

"You 'eard the latest? Courier from Port Galaén got himself attacked on the road yesterday."

"What? That's the third one this month? Who'd he say done it?"

"Highway bandits, he said. Though it was hard to hear him properly on account of the missin' teeth."

"Pneumos save us."

"No, Pneumos save *me*."

Georgie, the shop owner, made this last statement as he sidled over to join their conversation.

"Upstandin' merchants like m'self are bein' asked to pay protection money to rovin' *guardsmen* to ensure our suppliers make it through." He said this last with a twist of his lips that yielded the desired sputters of outrage from his companions.

"Probably the same guardsmen doin' the attackin' in the first place," growled the first man.

"But what choice do I have?" Georgie asked. "Without my goods, I'll be ruined. And it isn't like the Tiarna's good for anything."

All five nodded in agreement at this and Georgie turned to serve the next customer in line.

Danny felt his scowl deepen. Knowing how close to ruin so many of the shopkeepers in Abalás lived, it made a cold fury settle in his stomach to think of local gangs pushing them even closer to the edge.

Suddenly, Danny thought back to the dying trees of the ancient oak grove and shivered once more. They couldn't possibly be related, could they? Elliott had always warned him that chaos left its mark on more than just events and people. It could be felt and seen in the world around you—everyday abberrancies the summed to more than their parts.

After all, signs of the unraveling always preceded the destruction.

He'd have to bring this up with Elliott next time he saw him. The Legion needed to be told. Things seemed to be progressing even faster than they'd thought.

CHAPTER
EIGHT

The days passed slowly, filled with long hours spent listening to Elliott's stories as she helped him and Danny with chores around the farm. Keira was admittedly quite skittish around both. She'd never lived with men before and the ones her mom had brought around weren't exactly the most savory of characters. She spent the first few days tip-toeing around the two, watching warily for any sign of temper and ready to flee at the first sign of trouble. But Danny's quiet companionship and Elliott's ebullient enthusiasm soon soothed her nerves, at least a little.

Elliott in particular seemed to take his assumed role as mentor and instructor quite seriously. Their *lessons* began almost immediately, eager as he was to pass on to her all that he knew. A favorite activity was hunting for the herbs he used in his medicines and poultices. In the hours they'd spend trekking over the countryside in search of the desired flora, Elliott would regale Keira with stories of Loren—tales of invading conquerors, Regios and their loyal commanders, and warrior queens that charged at the head of mercenary armies. It often left Keira unsure of which stories were history and which legend, an objection Elliott would merely shrug off.

"My dear, we tell stories to understand who we are and how we came to be. History may inform the present, but our understanding is defined as much by fiction as by fact."

These tales were regularly interrupted by Keira's curious questioning as to the details of these warrior kings and queens, their lives, motivations, and ends—side tangents that Elliott clearly relished. He would frequently interrupt these ancient tales with his own practical knowledge about the various plants and animals they encountered and workable instruction for their use and care. Though Keira was initially wary, she'd always been an eager student, and here she found an opportunity to fall back into that old, familiar role. She hoarded information with a fervor, squirreling away every new insight, eager for anything that might help her better understand this strange new world, anything that might one day help her escape.

Elliott really did have an impressive library that filled the living room shelves of the otherwise humble cottage—histories detailing the conquests of the Marian Empire, myths and fables of the Lorenan uplander, Legion tomes on the practice and study of pneumonancy.

What's more, Keira found solace in this old comfort, curling up with a book in hand. While Danny and Elliott were busy training, Keira would keep to a safe distance, eyes devouring tales of the rise and fall of empires and the hopes and dreams of the Lorenan people.

But even as she filled her days with books and chores, she treaded water against the tug of depression that threatened always to pull her beneath the waves. And day after day, she found herself staring off in the river's direction. She watched as the treetops turned from green to gold, waiting and hoping beyond hope.

For what? That her mother might suddenly turn up? That Molly would stumble from among the trees?

She knew that hope was pointless. She understood that the more days passed, the less likely their sudden appearance became. Even so, she hoped.

It was on just such a day that she found herself perched by the river's edge just south of the cottage, twirling her fingers in the tiny eddies of water as a crisp breeze blew strands of hair away from her face. She shivered, staring up at the sky as she wondered how long until the weather turned and fall shifted into winter's grip.

A rustling from the woods behind her caught her attention and she slowly turned her head, expecting to see Danny or Elliott emerge and summon her to dinner.

She froze.

Breath coming in tiny gasps, she stared at the hulking mass of fur that sidled its way down to the riverbank in front of her.

It looked like a bear, but was bigger than anything Keira had ever seen at the zoo. This creature's shoulders were massive and even on all fours, it stood nearly as tall as she did. And it seemed . . . wrong.

The creature seemed almost disfigured, one shoulder arched high above the other. Its beady eyes met hers and Keira gasped at the blood that encircled each pupil. She began to shake as a layer of foam dripped from its lips, a steamy cloud billowing from its nostrils with each snorting breath.

Keira's heart hammered in her ears and her breathing picked up, each one tearing at her chest. She desperately racked her brain for everything she knew about bears and how to survive if confronted by one. Weren't you supposed to punch them in the nose? Or was that sharks? Why on earth had she not paid more attention to the discovery channel?

As her mind raced, her hand spasmed against the pebbly riverbank, searching for something, anything she might use as a weapon. Yet the biggest rock she could find was smaller than her palm, and she had the sneaky suspicion it wouldn't exactly stop the beast in its tracks.

With every second that passed, the creature grew closer and closer as it neared the riverbank. She had to do something . . . and *now*.

With a force of will that surprised even her, Keira managed to get both legs underneath her and she watched the bear closely as she slowly rose to her feet, bracing for any sign of a charge.

Inch by inch, she backed away, eyes locked on the bear with every step. Her arms rose in a placating motion.

You can have the river, friend. It's all yours. Just please *let me leave.*

The bear stopped its advance and eyed her with interest. *That's it,* she thought as she continued to inch backward. *Just let me be.*

Then, in a moment of profoundly bad luck, Keira's foot caught on the edge of a larger rock and she let out a tiny cry as it rolled painfully to one side. She caught herself before her face smashed into the rocky ground, ignoring the fire that raced from her palms at the impact.

She glanced up just in time to see the bear's ears perk up at her cry. Then it lowered its head and charged.

Panic coursed through her, lighting every muscle on fire as she scrambled to her feet.

She ran.

Ignoring the lance of pain that shot from her foot with each step, she raced forward. Fueled by adrenaline, she didn't stop to think, to look back, or consider the very high likelihood that she was about to die . . . again.

Because at that moment, she knew she wanted to live. Whatever this new life was and no matter how strange this world might be, she wanted to live.

No sooner did she have this realization that her foot buckled and she slammed into the ground with a cry as her knees crunched against rock. She rolled to one side, clutching at the ankle that now felt engulfed in flames—just in time to see the hulking mass of the bear barreling toward her.

She stared at it, momentarily at a loss. This was it. She was really about to die again. Would she see her mom? Molly? She didn't know how this second life was supposed to work, or indeed this second death. But she was . . . angry.

This wasn't how it was supposed to end, not like this. Not mauled by a bear while she stared helplessly back. Gritting her teeth, her fingers closed around a nearby rock. No, if she was going to die again, she'd go out fighting this time.

The sudden whistle of an arrow cut through the air and Keira's head shot up just in time to see the animal's thunderous roar. An arrow jutted out from the beast's shoulder. It hadn't fallen, but the impact had momentarily stopped its charge. Its eyes once again fell on Keira as it swung its head from side to side, nostrils flaring dangerously.

Keira scrambled backwards on the rocks, trying to regain her footing as the bear took one step and then another toward her. Then suddenly, a strong grip caught her under one arm and Keira's gaze shot up to meet Danny's tense green eyes.

"Can you walk?" He asked, eyes already leveled back on the bear, bow at the ready.

"I—I think so."

"Alright, then we're goin' to very slowly back away. Whatever you do, *don't turn* and *don't run*."

Keira swallowed, flattening her palms against her legs to keep them from shaking as she did as he instructed, wincing with every ounce of weight she put on her injured foot.

The bear watched them for a moment, considering, before turning to lick at its wounded shoulder.

"Just keep backing away," Danny whispered, bow still at the ready as they inched backward.

"You sure you don't want to try shooting it again," Keira hissed, eyeing the monstrous creature.

"And get it charging?" He snapped. "No thanks, sweetheart."

Keira scowled back at him. "It was just a thought."

"Got it. Thanks."

At that moment, the creature's head swung back to them. Beady eyes fixed them with a glare as thin lips pulled back from a low snarl.

Keira's breath caught in her throat, and she felt beads of sweat line her brow.

"Ok, now what?" she demanded in a strained whisper. Danny swore in a low voice. Keira's eyes shot to his, not exactly finding that response comforting.

And then it charged.

"RUN!"

Keira didn't need to be told twice.

Sprinting for the treelike every step sent shocks of pain reverberating up from her leg, and every second she felt her pace slow incrementally. Danny's head whipped around, taking in all this in an instant. His lips pressed together in a thin, determined line.

He stopped.

"Keep going," Danny said grimly, eyes fixed behind her. "I'll do my best to hold it off."

"You'll—WHAT?" Keira gasped, reaching him a moment later. "You can't — I can't just—"

"Go, Keira." Danny snarled, fitting an arrow to his bow. "There's nothing more you can—"

A boom thudded just behind them. Keira felt the shockwave first and dropped to her knees. Danny's arm came around her and he covered their heads as a shower of rocks rained down on them.

"What the—"

"Keep your head down," Danny hissed. But Keira peered through the gap of his arm to see the earth collapse back in place. The creature was still there but had halted in its tracks. Its eyes met hers and a low snarl peeled from behind its lips. Keira swallowed and the creature moved.

No sooner had she opened her mouth to shout a warning, than a wall of rock erupted from the river bank, the earth itself jutting upward toward the sky. It held its position for just a moment before crashing back to earth sending another roar and shockwave barreling down on them.

This time the creature turned and ran.

A low trembling breath escaped through Keira's teeth as she

scrambled to her feet, hands shaking as she spun to look for the source of the eruption.

Elliott strode towards them, with all the air of an English gentleman out for a stroll. A light breeze ruffled his auburn hair and he shot them a wide grin.

"Seems *you* two needed a hand."

Danny snorted and rolled his eyes. "*Show off.*"

Elliott merely shrugged. He strode past them to inspect his handiwork, kneeling beside the massive mound of earth.

"That thing should never have been here, Elliott," Danny began. "Not this far from the mountains. And did you see its face? There was something seriously—"

"That's *enough*, Danny." Elliott cut him off with a look and Danny's mouth snapped closed. They stared at each other for a long moment before Danny's gaze dropped to his feet. Keira's eyes darted between Danny and Elliott, trying to read the heavy silence that had fallen between them.

"Anyone going to explain what exactly just happened?" She demanded.

They both blinked in surprise as they turned her direction. Danny chuckled at her expression.

"*That* was pneumonancy."

Keira gaped at him. "So I take it there's more to it than just boiling water."

Danny laughed aloud at that.

"You have no idea."

Keira shook her head, reeling at the implications, even as the adrenaline oozed from her body, leaving her exhausted and vaguely nauseated.

"Here, let me see that ankle."

Keira blinked up at him in surprise.

"It's fine," she protested, even as she winced with each step.

"Mmm Hmm." Danny replied, thoroughly unconvinced. He tugged her down to sit on the nearby log and she reluctantly agreed. Gently, he tugged her boot off and she bit her tongue against the whimper that would have decimated any last vestiges of her pride. Danny inspected every inch of her foot, gently flexing and extending it at the ankle.

"Does this hurt?" He asked, pressing on various bony prominences.

She shook her head. "Not unless I move it."

Danny nodded, apparently satisfied with that answer.

"I don't think it's broken, probably just a bad sprain."

Keira nodded, biting her lip, before adding, "Thank you for back there."

Danny glanced up at her, head cocked at an angle.

"You're welcome." Then he paused, surveying her thoughtfully. "You know, you might reconsider training with us. Might make you feel better. I mean, this world isn't like yours—or mine, for that matter. It's rougher, more dangerous. And there aren't exactly coppers to call when things go wrong. You might feel better, more . . . capable, if you could protect yourself."

"I don't know," Keira muttered, thinking of the complex drills she'd seen Danny and Elliott rehearsing in the training field. "I've never been much for physical stuff and I avoided sports like the plague. I mean, I only went to PE because it was required . . ." She trailed off, blushing as she caught Danny's slow, sidelong grin. She was doing it again, she realized—the mouth leaking.

Danny quickly hid his smile, all business again.

"We'll start simple, I promise."

"All right," Keira said warily. "I guess I can give it a try."

CHAPTER

NINE

"I'm sorry, you want me to do *what*?"

Keira and Danny squared off on opposite sides of the training yard. It had been a long morning already and even the horses had sidled over to watch the excitement.

Danny rolled his eyes at Keira's outburst and said in a long-suffering tone, "I *told* you, we're practicing takedowns."

Keira snorted and crossed her arms over her chest, hoping he didn't notice the flush she could already feel creeping over her cheeks. "Yes, I heard that part. What I'm less clear on is why exactly I would pull you on top of me? Aren't I trying to get away in this scenario?"

Danny pinched the bridge of his nose, glancing heavenward in silent supplication.

Keira felt her jaw clench. How very like him to claim *she* was the one causing problems.

"We've been over this. The point is to keep your opponent off balance. Their natural inclination will be to keep their distance, at least initially. By closing the distance, you throw them off and simultaneously take the impact out of their strikes. It's hard to hit someone who's right up against you."

Keira weighed his words, eyeing the hard ground of the training yard with distrust. Danny sighed.

"Here I'll do you first."

"*Excuse* me?" The words were out of her mouth in an instant, and she regretted them immediately. Danny's sun-freckled cheeks darkened slightly but he kept his voice level.

51

"I would like to *demonstrate*."

Keira felt like crawling in a hole, but managed a small nod.

"Excellent," Danny said, back to business.

"Square off toward your opponent. They've already got one hand on your shirt, so you're going to keep it there." Danny grabbed her wrist and fixed it solidly against his shoulder. She gripped the rough homespun fabric instinctively, nervously watching as he grabbed a fistful of her shirt with the other hand.

"Now you're going to do a controlled fall backwards, pulling them along with you."

He gave her a sharp tug and she stumbled forward as he somehow landed gracefully on his back. Meanwhile, she flopped forward, only failing to land on top of him because of the foot he'd shot up to wedge against her hip.

What the—

"Now you just sweep your other leg through."

What followed was a complex maneuver involving his arm hooking around her free leg. Before she knew it, she'd been tossed onto her side and held in what Danny called a "side guard."

By the end, Keira was sore, dirt-covered and decidedly *not* enjoying herself.

"Alright, now you give it a try."

Keira stared at him. Was he serious? She'd barely understood the move as it was happening. There was no way she could emulate it.

"That is, unless you need a break."

Danny's innocent smile was a challenge and Keira felt her spine stiffen. She narrowed her eyes back at him.

"Nope, I'm fine."

"Good to hear."

Refusing to back down, Keira squared off in front of him and braced one hand on his shoulder and the other clutching the sleeve of the arm gripping her collar.

Now or never.

Keira gave a light tug.

Danny didn't budge, his mouth twisting into a smirk.

"You'll have to put a little more muscle in it, sweetheart," he drawled in his thick Boston accent. "I'm a big lad."

Keira scowled up at him.

I'll show you muscle, sweetheart.

Squaring her shoulders, she gave a giant heave, and flopped backward. Caught off guard, Danny stumbled toward her and she just managed to get her foot up in time to prevent him flattening her completely—catching him mid-groin.

Danny grunted, his face contorting as if he'd just swallowed a lemon. "A little . . . to the *left*," he said through gritted teeth.

Oh. Dear. God.

"I'm sorry!" Keira squeaked, feeling her face turn scarlet. She immediately readjusted her foot position.

"It's. Fine." Danny hissed, pursing his lips.

In that moment, Keira wanted nothing more than to sink through the very earth.

But she refused to give him the satisfaction.

"I mean, whatever works, right?" She gave a nervous laugh that quickly faded as his eyes narrowed darkly. "You know, in a fight."

"Mmmm hmmm."

It took the better part of an hour, filled with multiple failed attempts that landed her square on her rear on the training yard floor. But through stubborn persistence and sheer will, Keira finally figured out the takedown. And when she flipped Danny onto his side in a plume of dust, she practically crowed with delight.

"I did it!" She cried, inordinately pleased with herself despite her still uncanny resemblance to a newborn colt.

"You did," Danny said, trying and failing to keep a straight face as Keira did a little happy dance.

"Laugh all you want," Keira declared, waggling her finger at him as his lips twitched suspiciously into a smile. "But I took down someone twice my size today and you will not take that from me."

"I wouldn't dream of it. You ready for the next one?"

Keira's face immediately fell and Danny snorted aloud at his expression.

"Only teasing, sweetheart. I say we earned ourselves some dinner, don't you?"

Keira readily agreed and the two of them headed inside to the dinner they could smell wafting out from the open windows. And to her surprise as much as anyone else's, Keira found herself . . . content. Not happy necessarily, but a little less wretched. And for now, she decided that was a win.

TEN

Keira was certainly determined. Danny would have to give her that. If he was being honest, he'd expected her to give up a long time ago. If he was being *really* honest, he'd hoped she would. Then maybe Elliott would see that some sort of mistake had been made, that this wary-eyed girl without an inch of muscle on her couldn't possibly be his cantor.

To be sure, she seemed nice enough—helping out around the farm and smiling at Elliott's admittedly terrible jokes. But *nice* didn't help anyone when the bombs started dropping. Danny knew that better than anyone.

But still she persisted. No matter what he threw at her—hand to hand combat, land navigation, horseback riding—all the essentials skills to surviving in Loren. She faced every challenge head on, usually with a fair amount of blood, sweat, and swearing. But hey, he was the last one to judge on that account.

He had to admit he was impressed. She wouldn't be living off the land any time soon, but she certainly wasn't the delicate flower he'd initially pegged her for.

So when the time came to head into Abalás for supplies (not to mention following up on the rumors of increased bandit activity in the area), he decided it was time for round two. It had taken some serious needling but he'd finally convinced her to venture back into town with him—to see and appreciate Abalás for herself.

It had seemed like a good idea at the time.

But as the two of them rode side by side through the forest road, the heavy weight of silence descended. In vain, he wracked his brain for something, anything to say to fill the awkward void. But the two of them didn't exactly have much in common. After all, she was a college girl born half a century after he'd gotten himself killed on a war-torn battlefield half a world away. And she was a *reader* to boot. What did readers even talk about? Books? Something told him his limited memories of high school English wouldn't serve him well in actual conversation. So he fell back on the next best thing.

"You know, the sorrel are really biting this season. Fry 'em just right and they're passable for a nice mackerel."

Keira turned to him, blinking repeatedly.

Fishing? That was the best he could come up with? Danny felt like smacking his head against the nearest tree, but didn't think that would add much to what he was sure was her rapidly diminishing view of his intelligence.

"Hmm," Keira replied, the sound a full octave above her normal speaking range.

Yep. She definitely thought he was an idiot.

"So um, read any good books lately?

Keira's eyebrows shot up nearly into her hairline.

"Do you read?"

Crap.

"I mean . . . I *can* read."

Brilliant. Absolutely brilliant.

"I actually just finished Elliott's copy of Birth of an Empire: History and Myth. It was all about the first Marian Emperio. Turns out there's a lot of similarities with the Romans in our world. Similar culture, political ambition, even weaponry."

"That sounds . . . interesting."

Keira cocked her head and eyed him with amusement. He could feel his collar growing hot.

"I take it books aren't high on your list of pastimes?"

Danny snorted. "Not exactly."

"So, what do you like to do? You know, when you aren't teaching me how *not* to impale myself on a sword."

Danny met her smile with a relieved grin of his own.

"I don't know. I enjoy being outside with the horses, I suppose, training with Nazor, fishing on the river." He shrugged, feeling suddenly self-conscious.

"Pretty good for a city boy," Keira teased.

Danny chuckled. "You're tellin' me. That's honestly what I enjoyed most about the war—if *enjoy* is even the right word."

Danny shrugged, trailing off self-consciously. But when he glanced over at Keira, she had turned completely around in her saddle to watch him—face filled with genuine interest.

"What was it like? I've read about World War II in my history books but never—" She started, then blushed. "I'm sorry. Is that a rude question?"

Danny shrugged again. "I don't mind. I've been here in Loren for about a year now, so things are less . . . fresh. Makes you remember more of the good stuff, I suppose."

Then he chuckled. "World War II, huh? I suppose that makes sense. For us, it was just *the war*. I was glad to go, don't get me wrong. Happy to do my part. But—"

His felt his voice trail off and he shook his head, avoiding Keira's curious gaze.

"There was so much death, Keira. And it would hit you out of nowhere. Inching our way through the French countryside, the Germans fought us for every foot of ground gained. And the towns we'd pass through were utterly destroyed. Every day we'd make it a little farther, just enough to uncover some fresh horror."

Danny swallowed and he shook his head, the words having fled as quickly as they'd come. He never talked about the war. Elliott and Nazor never asked. After all, they both knew what it was to hide from ghosts.

"I'm sorry," Keira said quietly. "I shouldn't have asked. We don't have to talk about it."

Danny glanced at her and shrugged. "It's all right. Good for me to talk about, I suppose. Because it happened, right? And the past tends to fester when ignored for too long."

Keira nodded and said nothing and they rode in silence for a long while. Then out of nowhere she asked, "What's Nazor like, anyway? You mentioned she was due back any day."

Danny chuckled. "Nazor is best . . . experienced."

Of course, Keira was far from satisfied with *that* answer. Keira peppered him with questions and so they spent the rest of the ride chatting about Nazor, her trip to Port Galaén, and the new training regimen she'd have planned for her arrival. But when the conversation turned to the mysterious Legion, Danny fell quiet. He merely shrugged at her questions about the organization or its purpose, claiming ignorance and skirting any deeper probing. It was true, he didn't know much about the Legion, but he also wasn't about to get into a discussion of cantors and grounders and whatever else was about to pop into her head. Now was definitely not the time. Luckily, she accepted the change in topic. But as he watched her sidelong, he was almost certain she was growing suspicious.

As they rounded a fork in the road to see the Western Road into town, Keira's nervous chatter only increased and he could see her shifting uncertainly in her saddle as the passerby nodded to the two of them.

"Just think of it as a village like any other." Danny murmured, eyeing her sidelong as her knuckles whitened against the reins. "Seriously, relax. You're making the horses nervous."

Keira snorted, but his words had their intended effect and he watched her finger loosen on the reins. Still, they'd probably have better luck on foot.

And so they dismounted, leading their horses by the reins as they made their way through the village toward the market square. Along the way, Danny stopped to point out the laughing children playing a game of Karvesh with carved wooden hourglasses that they tossed back and forth, carefully balanced on the string joining the river reeds they held in each hand. Keira stopped, enthralled, before a galout player bent awkwardly over the many-stringed instrument—utterly focused as he sent peals of lyrical melody dancing into the afternoon air.

With amusement, Danny watched as Keira's nerves slowly gave way to curiosity and finally to wonder. When she broke into applause at the conclusion of the galout player's song (earning a flourishing bow and surprised glances from passerby), Danny found himself smiling in earnest. There was just something about seeing this world through her eyes, full of wonder and excitement, always eager to learn and understand. It made him appreciate the home he'd found here all the more—far different from the one he'd left, but special all the same.

Danny left Keira outside with the horses while he stepped inside the general store to fetch the supplies they needed. When he returned, Keira was staring curiously at a woman across the street. She was draped against an open doorway, her flowing flaxen locks spilling over one shoulder. She was dressed similarly to the other women in a single piece of cloth draped across her shoulder, wrapped numerous times around her middle, and artfully draped in full skirts. But the edges of this woman's skirts folded back up to tuck into the large belt at her waist, showing off her bare legs in an almost taunting fashion. When she started whistling and fluttering her eyelashes at Danny, he quickly steered Keira in the opposite direction. She laughed openly at the deep shade of crimson he could feel stretching to the tips of his ears.

As they walked, Danny settled into his role as her personal teacher and tour guide, finding it surprisingly enjoyable. He told Keira all he knew about the people and buildings they passed, trying to give her a genuine sense of the community she'd entered. He explained the culture of Abalás, how its reliance on both the fishing and logging industries competed with the merchants' emphasis on the river trade, bringing small-town sensibilities into conflict with the wiles and whims of city life. When they passed robed men and women in various shades of color, Danny explained how most people in Loren worshipped Pneumos, the goddess of order.

"Pneumos as in pneuma? Like what Elliott uses?"

"Yeah, but most don't fully understand the connection. Each of the robe colors represents a different sect. I'm sure you can imagine, with something as vague as 'order,' everyone who takes the time to think about it somehow finds their own interpretation."

Keira nodded thoughtfully.

"What?" Danny challenged, knowing her well enough by now to be deeply suspicious of her silence. Keira shrugged and when Danny's brows crept further up his forehead, she sighed.

"I'm just trying to figure out what to make of this *goddess*."

"What do you mean?"

"I mean, I was never much for religion back in my world—too busy studying science, I guess. But even I have to admit, science doesn't exactly explain all of *this*."

She gestured broadly to the bustling village around them. Danny nodded, considering.

"I was raised a good Catholic boy, so I guess I just expect a fair amount of mystery in life. Why do things happen the way they do? Why do some survive and others don't?"

He shrugged, but from the corner of his eye saw Keira's jaw tighten. He shook his head.

"I don't have great answers, and I expect I never will. But what I do know is there must be a reason for it all, some purpose we fulfill by being here."

Keira's brow furrowed.

"What makes you so sure?"

Danny shrugged.

"I don't know. Some things you just know, yeah?"

Keira nodded sharply, eyes fierce.

"Like I know my Mom's still out there."

Danny blinked, taken aback. Then nodded slowly, memories of the car perched on a ledge and tumbling over filling his mind. He couldn't tell her, not yet. She needed hope, needed something to cling to.

"Yeah," he said, voice slightly hoarse. "Like that."

As they rode back in silence, Danny found his eyes drifting over to her profile. He still had no idea how this ill-prepared girl was supposed to survive in this world. But there was something about her, a curiosity combined with enthusiasm and determination that made him think she just might pull it off. And what's more, he found himself hoping very much that she would.

CHAPTER

ELEVEN

Keira spent the next few weeks in a state of cautious optimism. For every unpleasant realization she had about her new life —the complete absence of running water chief among them —a new discovery helped to reignite her natural positivity. She spent her days outside, helping Danny with the chores, surprising even herself with the interest she took in caring for the animals—horses, primarily, but also the chickens and milk cow they kept. The friendly barn cat, Mildred, made a pleasant surprise as Keira cleared out the hayloft. She found the cat carving out a nest that Danny predicted would soon be filled with mewing kittens.

Yet even these distractions were often not enough to keep Keira's mind from wandering back to the world she still couldn't quite believe was really gone. Some days, the misery of her situation completely overwhelmed her, and she could feel the wall she'd carefully constructed around the memories of her former life, and her mother most of all, crumble.

Oddly enough, Danny seemed to possess the uncanny ability to sense when this was happening. He could tell almost instantly when it was all becoming a bit too much. At these times, he seemed to make it a personal mission to distract her, keeping her mind focused solely on the present and out of its own dark crevices. On these days, they'd spend long hours after the chores were through exploring the woods and riverside in and around the house. The woods fascinated Keira, and she'd happily spend her time admiring the babbling brooks, where tiny frogs leaped out and kissed her toes as she marveled at the felled trees with their drooping moss beards strung low as they reclined against their neighbors. These places came alive to Keira, and for the first time in what felt like months, she felt herself truly relax. She breathed the cool, moist air in deeply as she let the sun's rays, tinted auburn from their journey through the changing foliage, wash over her face.

It was late morning, a few days after her trip into Abalás, when Keira and Elliott returned from an expedition in search of flygrass, an herb Elliott needed for a tea used to break a fever, to find a strange wagon in front of the house. Keira was instantly nervous, unsure who would visit, but Elliott barely noticed her questioning look. His burst into an earsplitting grin. His strides suddenly doubled, and Keira had to jog to keep up as he strode the hundred yards remaining to the house's front door.

A tall, dark-skinned woman met him, her traveling cloak draped over leather armor and hand resting easily on the hilt of a sword Keira guessed to be nearly as tall as herself. The woman met his whoop of laughter with a small smile of her own, her dark eyes crinkling at the edges. Elliott wasted no time at all and swept her into his arms, spinning her around and laughing at her sharp protest. He robustly kissed her on the mouth before returning her to her feet. She growled a reproach at him, straightening her mail tunic as she feigned affront at the indignity, betrayed only by the smile that still tugged insistently at her lips. Her eyes then fell on Keira and regarded her intently.

"So this is the new cantor you sent word of."

The woman had a low, velvety voice that belied her fearsome exterior. Her accent was almost British but had more of a lyrical quality that Keira couldn't quite place. She held Keira's gaze steadily, then smiled. "I am Chinazor Onodugo, but you may call me Nazor." The woman's gaze never faltered from Keira's . . . assessing. For what, Keira had absolutely no idea.

Elliott draped an arm casually over the woman's shoulders, a feat made more difficult by the fact she was nearly as tall as he was. "Keira, meet Nazor, my grounder, and Danny's other mentor."

Keira noted nervously that the woman stood a full head and shoulders above herself, a daunting figure decked in armor, her head haloed by a thickly braided bun that only added to her intimidating height. Keira shifted nervously from one foot to the other, regarding warily this woman she'd heard so many impressive stories about.

Danny suddenly appeared in the doorway and ran over to join

them. Keira was momentarily freed from the woman's steely gaze as she turned instead to address Danny.

"And you, have you kept up with your drills, as I asked?"

Danny smiled sheepishly back at her. "Come on, Nazor, you have to admit it's been a bit out of the ordinary here, what with getting Keira settled and showing her around."

"Indeed?" Nazor cocked her head at him, a severe look in her eye. "And how will you explain your distraction to the bandits that catch you unawares next time you take the Eastern Road? Never mind then. I'll just have to get you back in shape myself."

Danny's mouth twisted slightly at that, but Nazor continued, unheeding, "And with the three of us drilling, we can start learning larger group tactics."

Nazor's smile seemed genuine now, obviously pleased with these plans. But her statement caught Keira's attention.

"Three of us? You mean I'll be learning, what, sword fighting?"

Danny grinned at her, and Nazor gave her an even look. "Why, of course. I'm sure Elliott has explained the very real dangers that inhabit Loren."

Keira smiled ruefully. "One encounter with a hungry bear was enough of a warning."

Nazor raised her brows.

"And the human dangers?"

Now Keira's brows raised, this time at Elliott, who quickly clarified, "Well, of course we discussed them, but, I mean, we hardly wanted to scare the poor thing right off."

Nazor merely roll her eyes as she turned back to fix Keira with a measuring look. "As I'm sure you've seen, Loren differs greatly from where you come from. There are laws here, yes, meant to keep the citizenry safe. But those who would flout them do so with little fear of repercussions. Every individual is charged with their own defense, and I would never dare to travel alone with such cargo . . ." She motioned at the cart behind her, filled with packages and baskets, not to mention the cow tied to the back. ". . . were I not able to defend myself and my property. Besides," she said offhandedly, "our work requires more than the average amount of endangerment."

"Your work?" Keira asked. Was she finally going to figure out what exactly this mysterious Legion actually did in Loren?

Nazor smiled slightly at her, clearly reading the direction of her thoughts, if not their actual content. "Yes, our work, the nature of which you will discover in good time. As for now, all you need to know is that it requires our ability to move freely through the country without fear of harassment."

Keira felt the corner of her mouth twist ruefully as she glanced at Danny, who shrugged amicably. He was clearly no help. Didn't he ever wonder about this mysterious "work" they'd seemingly been volunteered for? *Apparently not*, she decided.

"Besides, I'd assume you'd like to feed yourself," Nazor continued, eyebrows arched pointedly, "and that you'd like meat to occasionally grace the menu. How's your archery?"

Keira didn't bother to reply. This woman clearly knew full well she'd never touched a bow or arrows in her life. Even the hand to hand combat Danny had been teaching her was progressing slowly. This entire exchange was starting to seriously get on her nerves.

Nazor's smile widened. "Well, that'll be the first lesson then, once we get these supplies unpacked." She turned and began unhitching the packhorse from the cart. Danny cleared his throat pointedly, and she turned to look at him.

"Aren't you forgetting something?" Danny asked, eyes twinkling. Nazor paused for a moment before suddenly remembering what he was referring to.

"Oh, yes! I did have one thing to show you first," she told Keira. "Come with me."

The three of them followed Nazor around the side of the stables to the large pasture they let the horses graze in. Keira heard Elliott whistle long and low, and she shielded her eyes against the sun to get a better look at the prancing chocolate mare in front of her. She was smaller than Boyd, Danny's palomino gelding. But her tall haunches curved down her back in a sleek slope. She tossed her silken mane in greeting as she ambled over to them, allowing Keira to admire the high step of her gait.

"She sure is a beauty," Danny murmured, reaching out a hand to stroke the star on her forehead. Mesmerized, Keira reached out a cautious hand toward the horse's nose and was greeted by flared lips nuzzling her, clearly seeking treats.

"I bought her off an old Tramor come down for the fair; gave me a good price, too."

Keira felt Nazor's eyes on her but couldn't seem to tear her gaze from the mare's long, intelligent face.

"When Elliott sent word you'd arrived, I figured a small palfrey would suit you well. Mind you, you'll not be charging into any battles on her," Nazor warned, patting her own great black destrier, who'd sidled up to the fence in greeting. "But she'll serve you well for long hours of riding. She ambles, see, making her smooth as silk to ride. Good for beginners." Keira heard the teasing in her tone and turned to stare at her.

"You mean, sh-she's mine?"

Nazor regarded her long and hard. "In as much as any living soul belongs to another, she will serve you and serve you well. Mind you care for her in turn. She's a smart girl, and she'll know when she's being disrespected."

Keira rubbed the beautiful mare's neck and breathed, "Always. Isn't that right, Cerise?" Keira thought she saw Nazor's eyes soften as she nodded approvingly.

"A noble name. She's a mountain mare, you know," Nazor informed her. "She lives for roaming hills and clifftop trails, and she will rarely misstep."

Brushing off her tunic, Nazor then turned brusquely and motioned for them to follow her. "But first, we have supplies to unload, a midday meal to prepare, and a first archery lesson to conduct."

Keira wavered at the fence, not wanting to leave this beautiful creature that had only just found her, but she eventually turned and reluctantly followed the others back toward the wagon.

TWELVE

That day, Keira received a rude awakening as to the reality of truly studying the fighting arts. Her first lesson in archery left her with raw fingers and split knuckles as she learned first to string a bow, plucking and adjusting its tautness. She'd practiced again and again, nocking an arrow, hooking it with three fingers, drawing it back to her ear, and then holding, holding, and yet more holding.

Nazor was merciless, slowly pacing behind her to correct every inch of her stance, posture, and shoulder position. Meanwhile, her muscles trembled under the strain of trying to hold the bow taught. Nazor had directed Keira to a smaller recurve bow, its tips angling away from her in generous sweeps, for her to start with. Yet even with its smaller size, it still stood past her waist, and she could barely hold it at full draw for more than a few seconds, her back muscles seizing with the effort. Keira couldn't imagine actually having time to aim at anything. Nazor tsked her disapproval.

"A warrior should learn to shoot at least six times per minute, and from the back of a galloping horse, no less." Seeing Keira's dubious look, she amended, "You'll get there . . . eventually."

Keira had quietly hoped that her obvious ineptitude might spare her the promised hunting expedition, but no such luck.

"Even if you can't shoot, it'll still do you good to learn the woods."

"Danny's been showing me the woods. I've even learned how to set snares."

She hated herself a little for the note of pride that crept into her voice. She was rewarded by the hint of a smile that flashed across Nazor's face, soon replaced by raised eyebrows.

"Oya, very good. You can show me what you've learned, then."

Oh crap, Keira thought.

She glared at Danny, whose sudden racking cough sounded suspiciously like muffled laughter. He met her narrowed gaze with wide-eyed innocence, and she shook her head in exasperation, earning her an encouraging grin in return.

It didn't go quite as badly as she'd expected. Her simple noose snare had, to her delight, actually caught a small rabbit, and she felt herself flush with pleasure at the sight of her handiwork. The trouble came when Nazor asked to see her reset the trap.

Though she'd practiced tying the noose repeatedly with Danny, something about Nazor's dark, critical eyes made her fumble the knots. She could feel her ears burning with embarrassment. Then she balked when Nazor asked her to actually skin the rabbit she'd caught. She hadn't gone over this part with Danny yet, and she spent a few moments grasping in vain for memories of her semester in pre-med anatomy, following strict instructions on precisely the best way to skin a cat. Finally, she admitted defeat and asked Nazor to show her.

Yet even these mistakes couldn't sully the pride of gulping down big mouthfuls of the rabbit stew she'd helped provide herself. As they ate, Nazor gave them the highlights of her trip to Port Galaén.

"The Tramors had quite the variety this year. Apparently, the fair in Port Tuálath had a poor showing. Port Cála's racked with the blood sickness and so had to be avoided altogether. I got some wonderful prices." Nazor turned to Keira, who'd been nodding off over her stew, to clarify. "The Tramors are nomads who journey south from the Arid Lands to the north. They head a summer caravan that passes through Port Galaén on its way to the capital in Cr"d Eálas, far to the south. They're known for their horseflesh and steel weaponry."

Keira nodded sleepily, and the other three laughed before launching into a debate on the merits of Tramorian steel versus Cross Sea stonework. Keira remembered wondering dreamily how exactly one made weapons out of stone before fully nodding off. She fell into bed later that night, exhausted and aching to the bone but profoundly pleased with herself.

Maybe I can do this after all.

~

THE UNCEREMONIOUS SPLATTER of wet rags against her face jolted her from sleep.

"Up! Wash yourself!" a soft voice commanded, cutting through the darkness as if shouted. Keira sat bolt upright, blinking sleep from her eyes and squinting against the early dawn light to see Nazor's tall shadow framing the doorway to her attic room. Not waiting for Keira to finish rolling out of bed, she tossed her some soft buckskin leggings, a belted tunic with billowing sleeves, and small, flexible shoes with flat soles that bent easily down the middle.

"Five minutes. Meet in the drilling yard."

Then she was gone, leaving Keira blinking and wondering, not for the first time, what on earth she'd gotten herself into.

Outside in the crisp morning air, the sun was just beginning to rise, and dawn light glinted on the dew that brushed Keira's ankles, making her shiver. She found Nazor and Danny in the dirt practice fields by the horses' pasture. Danny smiled a greeting toward her in his typical, easygoing manner, while Nazor only grunted in acknowledgment.

I guess she's not a morning person, Keira thought, wondering why on earth she'd woken her up this early then.

Keira was surprised to see that the four horses stood near the fence, fully groomed. Their ears twitched toward the humans in interest. But when she turned to Danny questioningly, he merely shrugged.

"Nazor helped me. We figured you could use the extra bit of sleep after yesterday."

Keira turned in surprise toward Nazor. She'd done the chores for her? Keira was wondering if there might not be more to this woman than her gruff exterior suggested, when Nazor suddenly barked out, "Let's go!"

She took off at a slow jog around the practice field, and Keira fell in behind Danny, who immediately set about following Nazor. Their speed gradually increased until they were sprinting, and Keira soon found herself short of breath as she struggled to keep up with the others' much longer strides. Nazor then led them through short agility exercises that emphasized rapid side-to-side movements and short-distance sprinting. When Nazor called for a break about half an hour later, Keira was gasping for breath and doubled over. She gladly accepted the ladle Danny proffered from a large water bucket.

"How often do you do this?"

He smiled, still breathing easily. "Every morning. You get used to it."

Keira groaned, and Danny's laugh was cut short as Nazor barked that it was time to stretch.

Now this, Keira thought, *is more like it.*

She luxuriated in the languid stretches, massaging her poor muscles in delight. She could have cried when the stretches ended all too soon and Nazor handed her, instead, a stick.

"I figured I'd at least get a wooden sword," Keira muttered, eyeing the gleaming blade Danny drew effortlessly from its sheath. "This thing isn't even shaped like a sword."

In truth, it was closer to a small branch. But she still felt incredibly silly trying to mimic Danny's "on guard" position as Nazor paced around her, correcting every minute detail.

"Square your legs," she barked, rapping the back of one knee smartly with her staff.

"Right foot forward."

"Bend your knees!"

"Lean forward slightly . . . No, no, too much!"

"Keep to the balls of your feet, not resting on your laurels. Are you at ease or at the ready?"

When finally Keira had assumed a stance that satisfied Nazor, she turned then to her grip on the sword-stick. Nazor explained that a single-handed sword is not, in fact, meant to be death-gripped with your entire fist. Using her own sword to demonstrate, she showed Keira how to hold most of the sword's weight between the thumb and the first two fingers, while the remaining two curled loosely around the hilt, truly engaging only at the peak of a sword thrust.

"The balance of a sword is essential to proper control, and its center of mass should rest precisely at the hilt so it may be wielded deftly by just these three fingers," Nazor explained. "Now you try."

From the corner of her eye, Keira could see Danny working through an elaborate drill, stepping lightly and moving his sword in long, elegant sweeps. She looked at her own stick dubiously, but adjusted her grip and assumed the "on guard" position. Nazor roughly adjusted the angle of the stick's upward point so that more of Keira's right shoulder was protected before proceeding to demonstrate the other seven guard positions, designed to protect the head, shoulders, gut, and legs on both sides.

Keira then had to proceed quickly between them, producing the correct guard to the various attack names Nazor called out. Two hours later, Keira's arm ached, and she was fairly sure she had two good-sized knee bruises where Nazor's staff had seen fit to correct a lapsed stance.

"Do I actually get to learn those attacks at some point?" Keira asked finally.

Nazor smirked. "I assumed you'd want to first learn how to avoid being skewered before doing any skewering of your own."

"But how do I know how it all fits together?" Keira protested.

Nazor considered this, head cocked slightly, before calling Danny over from the tree-trunk dummy he was happily stabbing to death.

"You watch."

What proceeded next seemed to Keira a strange mix between dance, ritual, and assault. Nazor and Danny squared off and faced one another before both assuming the guard position. The exercise began with both advancing and retreating in seemingly choreographed unity. Neither mis-stepped, keeping a constant distance between them, with swords held at the ready but unmoving. Then, with no sign of preagreement, Nazor began barking out attacks mere seconds before her sword flashed with lightning speed at the aforementioned location.

"High!"

"Low!"

"Middle!"

"Thrust!"

Each swing was met deftly by Danny's block from the guard positions Keira had spent all morning learning, and he easily parried the rapid thrust to his middle as he twisted adroitly out of the way. Eventually, Nazor stopped announcing each swing before it occurred, and they quickly became more rapid, steel flashing as she whirled and spun toward Danny. He met each attack with a block that, with a flourish, transitioned effortlessly into the next attack.

They seemed well-matched. Nazor was an inch or so taller and quick on her feet, but Danny's incredible strength gave him a slight edge. Eventually, though, Danny blocked an overhead swing too close to his own hilt, and Nazor quickly moved in to grapple with his wrist, bracing his sword arm aloft while her blade flashed in a backward arc over and inward, stopping a mere inch from his exposed left side. Grinning ruefully, Danny yielded, and the sparring ended, with Keira left to marvel at the skill and ease with which they brandished their one-handed blades. She wondered if there was any way she'd ever be that good.

I will, she told herself. *I have to.*

Getting home meant finding the Legion and that mysterious library of theirs. But first . . . first she had to learn to survive.

THIRTEEN

With Nazor's return, Danny felt a new normal settle on the farm. Elliott was, of course, ecstatic to have Nazor home and the two of them were embarrassingly lovey dovey as usual. This seemed to take Keira by surprise, and Danny would often catch her eyeing the two with curiosity. Danny couldn't exactly blame her. He'd been equally thrown by their relationship when he first arrived. They were opposites in nearly every way. Elliott with his constant chatter, ebullient personality, and ready laugh. Nazor with her stoic reserve, narrow-eyed contemplation, and the rare twitches at the corner of her mouth that were her version of ecstatic delight. They were fire and ice, oil and water. Perfectly compatible and yet wholly different. Danny had long since stopped trying to make sense of it.

Unsurprisingly, Nazor's arrival had upended the careful balance Danny and Keira had struck and Nazor wasted no doubt before setting about to whip her new ward into shape. Sword fighting, hand to hand combat, and mounted maneuvers were just the start. To his surprise, Keira tackled every challenge head-on—no complaints, no protests, just steely eyed determination. After all, Nazor was nothing if not a trying taskmaster.

More than once Danny caught Keira dozing off at the dinner table or with a book perched on her lap by the evening fire. She was working hard each day, determined to gain Nazor's frosty approval and ending up utterly exhausted. He couldn't help but find it endearing and he would often chuckle to himself before nudging her awake and helping her up to bed, each step up the stairs bringing with it a fresh groan from her no doubt aching muscles.

And so their days passed in a flurry of activity as Nazor drove them both mercilessly in their training. Danny didn't mind, had actually missed his mentor's barking growl from across the training field, the warm ache in his muscles after a tough training session. He'd worked with Nazor for so long that he wasn't bothered by her gruff demeanor or growled instructions. But more than once he caught Keira's eyes blinking furiously after a sharp reprimand and he felt a tight squeeze in his chest as she'd clamber to her feet, not meeting either of their eyes.

She was definitely a crier. Whether angry or sad, happy or frustrated, tears seemed to be her body's default response. The first few times it had happened, he'd been extremely uncomfortable, and not to mention confused. He was an Army corporal for Pneumos' sake and the crying reflex had been all but drilled out of him back in basic. But there was something about Keira's tears, the way she'd furiously brush them aside, trying hard to hide them but unwilling to let them stop or slow her down. Nazor paid them precisely zero mind but Danny couldn't help the budding swell of pride in his chest as Keira barreled forward undeterred.

It was several weeks after Nazor's arrival when he found Keira grooming Cerise in the stables one afternoon. Her brows were knit tightly together as she picked apart a particularly stubborn knot in the horse's mane. Danny watched her, suddenly nervous. He shoved the thought away. He was being ridiculous.

"I have something for you."

Keira glanced up in surprise, face lighting into a broad grin when she saw him. He ignored the answering tiny somersault in his stomach.

"A present?" She asked in surprise. "For me? Is it some sort of Lorenan holiday everyone forgot to tell me about? Because I definitely got nothing for you all."

Danny rolled his eyes at her teasing and gestured toward a bench. When they were seated, he passed her the long, carefully wrapped package from his saddlebag.

Keira's eyes twinkled as her fingers sprang to the knotted twine of the wrapping. Danny chuckled at her eagerness.

Keira became suddenly still as she drew the polished short sword from its wrapping and she seemed to stop breathing. She held the blade lightly on the tips of her fingers as she stared wordlessly at the gleaming steel.

Danny rubbed a hand against the back of his neck, suddenly nervous as he watched her inspect the gift.

"The pommel should fit your hands better and it's weighted for a shorter arm length so it shouldn't tire you out as much."

Still, she said nothing and Danny felt a thin sheen of sweat form on his brow.

"I mean, you definitely don't have to use it."

His rambling trailed off as big blue eyes suddenly turned to meet his.

"You got this for me?" Keira breathed.

Danny only nodded, feeling his cheeks heat.

"No one's ever . . ." Keira's voice trailed off and she shook her head as if clearing it of unwelcome thoughts. "Thank you, Danny." She whispered, twisting her wrist to admire the gleam of sunlight in the blade's polished edge.

"You're welcome. You . . . you deserve it. This is rough stuff and you've been working really hard."

Keira blinked up at him, surprised. He felt his cheeks grow warm again.

"Don't get me wrong. Your stance is still garbage and you're slow as hell, but . . . you're gettin' there."

Keira snorted. "Gee thanks. To be fair, this isn't exactly the type of study I was expecting to be doing this fall."

Danny nodded. He knew that. She was way smarter than any girl he'd met back home. She'd been going off to university after all. He couldn't imagine it himself. College had been so far beyond his grasp growing up, never even a question, really.

"So why a doctor? How did you know that's what you wanted to be?"

Keira snorted. "Why? Girl doctors too radical for you, grandpa?"

Danny rolled his eyes. "There may not have been many women doctors in my time, but more every day, especially with all the young lads goin' off to the war. Even I could see it was only a matter of time."

Keira was quiet for a long moment as she stared out the window.

"I was seven when I broke my arm riding my bicycle down Thompson Hill. My Mom was hysterical, crying and carrying on. I mean, it didn't take much for my Mom to become hysterical, but this was a lot even for her. It didn't even hurt that much, honestly. Too in shock, I guess. Anyway, we went to the emergency room and I was honestly more embarrassed by my mom than anything. The doctor, well he saw the problem straight away and he sent her out into the hall while they set it. I just remember being so relieved. I didn't cry—not even a little. Afterward, he . . . well, he said I'd make a good doctor myself someday."

Keira's eyes darted toward his. "It must sound silly, I know. I just—"

"No!" Danny suddenly blurted, snapping his mouth shut at her surprised glance. "I just mean. It makes sense. You took care of your mom, after all."

At Keira's curious expression, Danny swallowed. He mentally cursed himself for saying too much. She didn't know about his dreams and something told him she wouldn't appreciate his strange insight into her life.

"I just mean, it being the two of you and all. I'm sure you both had to take care of each other."

Danny held his breath, watching for her reaction.

Keira swallowed, brows still furrowed, but she nodded slowly. "It's good to feel useful, I guess. To feel like my life means something. Or it did anyway . . ."

Keira's voice trailed off and Danny didn't miss the note of bitterness that colored her words.

"You still can, you know." He murmured. "Be useful. Do something important."

Keira didn't answer and he couldn't tell if she hadn't heard him or had just chosen to ignore him. But he didn't push it, choosing instead to sit quietly beside her in the fading evening light, thinking about the little girl with the broken arm and big dreams that now may never come true.

CHAPTER

FOURTEEN

Keira's days of training and studying flew by in a flurry. Her exhaustion prevented her from fully comprehending the nature or shape of time as it passed, but as surely as ever, pass it did. The days grew shorter and the nights longer. Leaves fell from trees as autumn arrived in full, just as it had in the world she'd come from. She found this a comfort amid the otherwise absurd novelty. Then one day, their morning drill practice was met with a white frost dusting each blade of grass. Shocked by the obvious reminder of passing time, Keira wondered if she was really making any progress here.

Maybe it was just the thought of finally feeling in control of some aspect of her life, but Keira couldn't wait to finally get her hands on a real sword. It wasn't exactly that she was a natural fighter—far from it, in fact. The closest Keira had ever come to organized outdoor recreation had been a once-weekly mandatory gym class, and even that she'd judiciously avoided. But there was an elegance to sparring that captivated her. From the practiced footwork to the graceful overhead arc of blades whistling through the air, the sight made Keira's stomach flutter. Meanwhile, she'd been stuck with repetitive drills for months now. She wanted to feel the heft of real steel against an actual opponent. The only problem was, Keira was absolutely terrible.

Nazor had told her as much, laughing outright when she'd asked at the end of month one when she would be ready for an actual opponent.

"Oya, slow down, little Keira," she said, shoulders shaking so much they bounced her long crown of braids up and down as she laughed.

Yet beyond any newfound appreciation for the martial arts, the one thing that Keira valued above all else was not making a fool out of herself. And since, as previously established, the physical realm was not exactly a strongpoint of hers, this left Keira with relatively few options. So determined to finally make progress, she spent the next few weeks waking up every day before the crack of dawn. Like clockwork, she would make her way out to the training yard with the sword Danny had so kindly given her and run through her drills. She practiced until she could have done them blindfolded and on stilts— probably.

While she knew she was no swordsman, after two months of training, Keira could proudly confirm that she not only sported five additional blisters on each hand, but she was ready. She was ready not only to use an actual sword, but also to take on an actual opponent. The way she saw it, it only did so much good to face off against an imaginary partner, running through endless lines of drill. A real partner, she knew, would be far less cooperative.

Unfortunately, Nazor didn't seem to agree. No matter how many times Keira asked for a definitive timetable as to when she'd be able to progress with her training, Nazor merely stated point-blank that she was nowhere near ready.

Doesn't she realize how far I've come? Keira wondered. *How hard I'm working? Why can't she give me a chance?*

Meanwhile, the initial wary cooperation she'd shared with Danny had bloomed into something akin to real friendship. They spent many afternoons in the stables doing chores and just . . . talking. She told him about her life moving every few months and the odd relationship she had with her mom. He still said little about the war, but she couldn't fault him for that. Instead, he'd told her about Boston, his mother and sisters, the grocery where he'd been working since his father's death. His face changed when he talked about them, became somehow softer. While the concept of siblings was far beyond her understanding, she better than anyone understood the ties of family. And she wondered if maybe, just maybe, Danny really would understand why it was she had to find a way home. Then he'd given her that sword . . .

Keira shook her head, ignoring the fluttering in her stomach at the thought of his kind gift, so precisely designed to match her height and abilities.

She still couldn't quite get over the thoughtfulness of the gesture —this boy who should by all rights view her with nothing but disdain, a city girl who didn't know the first thing about horses, combat, or sword craft. But somehow, incredibly, he didn't. He believed in her, believed that she could learn all she needed to not only survive in this strange world, but thrive. And after a lifetime spent charging ahead, willing a future that no else thought possible, that belief was tangible, soul-lifting, and no small thing.

Keira took a deep breath, willing the fluttering in her stomach to cease at the thought of Danny and his small kindnesses. Her mind drifted to the half-smile and twinkling gaze he seemed to reserve just for her. Keira leaned heavily against the chest of drawers.

Get a grip, she reminded herself. *This is all only temporary. You know better.*

But as much as she reminded herself of this, day by day the girl she saw in the bedside mirror each morning grew less familiar. This girl was strong, marked by hard edges where before there'd been only softness, her skin tanned and hair lightened by hours spent outdoors. But more than anything, it was the sharpness in her eyes, the confident tilt of her chin that told her she was becoming a different person, inside and out.

It was with this thought that she grabbed her satchel and scampered out her bedroom door, heading for the twisting staircase that would lead down to the main floor.

"She's not ready."

Keira froze, one hand on the bannister and ears pricking at the sound of Nazor's icy voice wafting through the cottage.

"She's not ready, and frankly I doubt she ever will be."

"Come, my dear. She's only just arrived. There's still time enough." This came to her in Elliott's gentle lilt.

"If it were just a matter of skill, that would be one thing. But the girl is too timid. She doesn't have the heart of a warrior. Perhaps Danny was right. Perhaps there was a mistake."

Keira's mouth gaped, the wind knocked out of her like she'd been punched in the stomach. She reeled backwards, steadying herself on the bannister as she fought the wave of nausea.

Perhaps Danny was right.

Nazor she could understand. Nothing she did ever seemed to be good enough for her. But Danny?

The sting of betrayal rippled through her and she swallowed against the tears she could feel springing to her eyes. She'd thought they were becoming friends, maybe . . . maybe even more. How could she have been such a fool?

What did you expect? The old voice reminded her. *You know better than to rely on anyone else.*

Keira closed her eyes, breathing deeply through pursed lips as she tried to settle the pounding in her ears. Downstairs, she could hear the voices fading as Nazor and Elliott moved their discussion to the kitchen.

Now was her chance.

Steadying herself, Keira stole down the stairs, boots gripped in one hand and stockinged feet silent on the old wooden steps.

She slipped through the front door and stood for a moment, just breathing in the crisp late fall air. It slowed her breathing and cooled her throbbing headache. But in the place of hurt and confusion, a budding fury rose.

What in the hell had she been killing herself over the last few months for? The daily training, filled with the endless drills and soul-crushing corrections. And after all that, she didn't have enough *heart*? Well, she would show them. She would show all of them.

Why do you care? A voice in the back of her head asked. *Aren't you leaving, anyway?*

She shoved the thought away as she stalked toward the training yard. She'd stayed to learn to survive, to confront the Legion, and find a way home. And when the time came to leave, it would be on her terms. No one else's.

CHAPTER

FIFTEEN

Keira's boots made a satisfying crunch on the frozen grass as she stalked toward the training yard, eyes fixed on Danny's blonde head as he unloaded equipment from the weapon's chest. He glanced up at her approach and gave her a wide, crooked grin that made her stagger slightly in her determined stomping.

"Morning Keira," he called. "How'd you sleep?"

Rallying her wits, Keira reminded herself that she happened to be quite pissed off at him.

"Fine," she snapped.

Danny blinked in surprise, brow furrowing as he took in her fuming appearance.

"You don't seem fine."

"Well, I am," Keira replied, voice dripping with sarcasm.

"Look, if you—"

"Danny," Keira barked, cutting him off. "If I said I'm fine, then I'm fine. Leave. It. Alone."

Danny said nothing to that, merely shrugged and turned back to unpacking the weapon's chest. Keira swallowed thickly.

"I—I'm going to spar with Nazor today."

Danny snorted. "Is that so?" He glanced up at her casually, freezing at the sight of her tight jaw and folded arms. His eyes narrowed. "You can't be serious. Keira, you're nowhere near ready."

Keira felt her chin dart out stubbornly.

"What do you care? This has all been one big *mistake* anyway, right?"

Danny blinked, brows knit together as he cocked his head in a look of confusion. He opened his mouth to respond, but was interrupted by the crunch of approaching boots. Keira turned to see Nazor and Elliott making their way toward the training yard.

Before Danny could say a word, Keira strode out to meet them.

"I want to try sparring." Keira declared, eyes never leaving Nazor's stern face. Nazor blinked, surprised, before cocking one eyebrow in a look of amusement.

"Indeed? You think you can remain on your feet this time? Danny has quite the reach with that longsword."

Keira swallowed, willing every fiber of her nerve into her words as she corrected.

"No, I want to spar with you."

Nazor's eyes narrowed and she was quiet for a long moment. Keira fought the flutter of nerves in her gut, but refused to look away. Something sparked in Nazor's eyes as she took in Keira's stiff necked obstinacy.

"Very well," she replied cooly. "Let's spar."

At her tone, Danny's head jerked up from the bootlaces he'd been securing, and he rose to his feet, brow furrowed.

"Nazor, I don't know if—"

He was silenced by the sharp-eyed glare Nazor shot his way. "If Keira says she's ready, then we must give her the chance now, mustn't we?"

Keira was so shocked by Nazor's sudden acquiescence that she barely had time to react when Nazor threw her a grip guard. Keira caught the leather object but nearly dropped it as she scrambled to attach it to the pommel of her shortsword. She swallowed hard and quickly tried to suppress the rising panic that already had her stomach churning. Pursing her lips, she raised her arms to the "guard" positioned and watched as Nazor lazily advanced.

You can do this, she told herself. *Just like you practiced.*

This was nothing like she'd practiced.

Nazor was on her in an instant, blade flashing as she called out commands.

"Right!"

"Left!"

"High!"

"Thrust!"

Keira staggered back, barely moving her arm quick enough to

counter each bone-shattering blow. She could feel her footwork beginning to falter, even as she tried to maintain the stances she'd spent so long perfecting. Nazor pressed on, her flashing blade merciless in its onslaught. Keira fell back, feet tripping over themselves as her body instinctively shied away from the glinting blade that flashed mere inches from her face as she desperately tried to parry.

Keira suddenly noticed the silence that had crept in on her consciousness, and she realized with a start that Nazor had stopped calling out attacks. Yet still her blade flashed, coming ever closer to Keira as her own arm moved slower and slower. A billowing wave of panic pulsed upward in Keira's stomach, and for a split second, she wanted to bolt. Convinced beyond reason that Nazor was truly about to skewer her, she wanted nothing more than to get the hell out of there.

And she might have, too, were it not for the rock that caught the edge of her foot. Her ankle rolled out from under her, and she fell backward. Air flew from her lungs in a rushing *oomph*. All she saw as she looked up was Nazor's figure silhouetted against the early morning sun. As the blade came arching down, Keira could only close her eyes, waiting for the sharp bite of steel she knew would follow.

It never did.

She lay there for a moment before opening one eye and then the other. The tip of Nazor's blade was mere millimeters from her face. Keira sucked in a whistling gulp of air and stared up in helplessness at Nazor's stern face.

"Yield," came the low, flat reply.

Hand trembling slightly, Keira raised her two fingers in the traditional gesture of surrender.

Nazor slowly withdrew, and Keira took Danny's offered hand as she climbed ungainly to her feet, ears burning as she refused to meet his eye.

"Is that what you had in mind? I'm not sure what I'd call that, certainly not sparring." Nazor's voice was flat, and Keira glanced up to meet her narrowed gaze, shame quickly giving way to righteous indignation. She felt her nails bite into her palm as her hands curled into fists.

"Well, you didn't have to throw me off the deep end. We could have, you know, worked up to it."

"You think the ruffians you meet on the road will be any more generous?" Nazor's words came out in a low hiss, her eyes narrowing even further. Keira shook her head, refusing to be intimidated.

"Of course not, but I'm here to learn, right? Well, how can I do that when it's all or nothing? Either I'm running through stick drills by myself or having my ass handed to me. Is there no sort of progression?"

Keira looked from Nazor to Danny, hoping for some validation. She found none. Danny avoided her gaze, and Nazor's look was cold and deadly.

After a moment's pause that seemed to stretch indefinitely, Nazor responded, voice flat. "I do not know what the world was like where you came from. But here we train how we fight. The enemy will give you no quarter, and neither will I. You will fail and fail often. That is the way of things. But one thing you will never, *ever* do, so long as you train with me, is *close your eyes*."

Nazor took a step closer to her, and Keira barely resisted the urge to step away.

"You will look death in the *face* when it comes for you. You will miss no opportunity to evade it should it arise. But if you cannot, you will face it bravely and unblinking. Or else you will never be fit to call yourself a Legionnaire."

Keira's indignation faded as quickly as it had come, and a hot shard of shame pierced her gut. She gritted her teeth, cheeks burning, but shook her head, refusing to yield even then.

"I never asked to become a stupid Legionnaire. All I ever wanted was to live my life in my own world. Your friggin' Legion brought me here, not me, Nazor."

And with that, Keira turned on her heel and stalked away, feeling the tears of humiliation she'd just managed to hold back slide down her cheeks.

CHAPTER

SIXTEEN

Danny found her in a small glade not far from the farmhouse. She heard the crunch of his footsteps over the fallen leaves, but refused to meet his gaze as he approached slowly from the side. From the corner of her eye, she could see him fold his arms, eyes squinting against the sun as he looked out over the water.

"It could have been worse, you know."

She didn't look up, focusing instead on massaging the bruises that were forming on her arms.

"Sure," Keira snorted. "She could have *actually* stabbed me. That would definitely have been worse."

Danny smiled, flopping himself down on the ground beside her, legs outstretched. He leaned back, face arched toward the sun. "She's not as bad as she seems."

Keira snorted again. "You mean she's not a terrifying monster? She's actually human?"

Danny chuckled. "Well, she scared me stiff when I first arrived, and I'd faced machine gun nests."

Keira cocked her head at him, eyeing him curiously. Until now he'd said little about the war, quickly changing the subject any time it came up.

"Machine guns?"

Danny nodded, a shadow crossing his face but fading as quickly as it had come. "Yes. Nasty buggers. I'd say I gave 'em a run for their money. But I suppose they had the last laugh." Danny paused, glancing at her before shaking his head. "1944. Nazor tells me if I'd

83

made it another year, I might have seen the end of the whole damn thing."

Keira kicked at the ground, avoiding his eyes. *1944? So he was, what, seventy years older than her?* The thought hurt her head, so she pushed it aside.

"I was overseas for three years, even made corporal. Though they were so desperate, I'm sure the only real requirement was holding a gun and time in uniform. Eventually, even that last one became unnecessary. I watched as boys I'd brought in, trained myself, all died. Same thing for their replacements. I was on my third or fourth cycle for some of 'em. Well, that's not something that leaves you."

Keira nodded. She could see that, could see the effect it had on Danny. Even an entire world away, she could see he still carried those scars.

"You've been here a year or so, right?"

Danny nodded.

"And I was a mess at first . . . just like you."

He grinned at her, and she scowled back at him.

"Is that why you thought I must have been a *mistake*?"

She shrugged at his confused expression. "I heard Nazor and Elliott talking. She agrees with you, by the way. Says I don't have the *heart* of a Legionnaire, whatever that means."

"Ahh," Danny replied, shooting her a look of sympathy. "Thus the apparent death wish this morning."

Keira rolled her eyes. "I didn't think she'd *actually* try to kill me. But yeah, I don't know how much more *heart* I can show. Can't you all see I'm working my butt off here?"

Danny considered her before nodding thoughtfully. "You've worked really hard, Keira. No one doubts that."

Keira's brows nearly reached her hairline and Danny sighed.

"It's just . . . there's a lot more to being a Legionnaire than sword fighting, you know. We have a mission here, a purpose. That's what we train for every day, the thing that drives us. Meanwhile, from what I can tell, you're still just trying to get home."

Keira swallowed, guilt gnawing at her stomach. Because he was right, she was just trying to get home. More than anything, she ached to see her mom again, and if learning to defend herself was what it took, that's what she'd do. She just hadn't expected to make friends along the way.

"I am sorry though," Danny added, pushing the flop of hair off his brow and smiling sheepishly. "I should never have called you a mistake."

Keira considered him for a long moment, willing herself to hold on to that righteous indignation she'd swaddled herself in, a barrier keeping everything else out. But she couldn't stay mad at Danny. With that toothy grin and those olive-green eyes, it was damn near impossible. Danny just had a way about him. He made her feel understood, like he accepted her, warts and all. He'd pass no judgment, which in Keira's experience was definitely not a given.

Keira rarely trusted men. Her life growing up with Tammy had taught her they were shifty and unreliable. They were only after one thing, and once they got it, they didn't stick around long. But Danny, well, he seemed different.

"Thanks," Keira said finally, ignoring the fluttering in her stomach as Danny rewarded her with a broad grin. "I mean, I can't really blame you. I am pretty hopeless with a sword."

Danny shrugged. "You'll get there. I'd never touched a sword in my life, barely even seen a horse, city boy that I was. And now, a year on, well, I make do." He shrugged, tousling the back of his hair.

"I don't know, Danny. I really *tried.* I worked so hard, every day, and with nothing to show for it. Anyway, Nazor clearly hates me. That much is obvious. I just don't think I'm cut out for this."

Danny's voice softened, glancing at her cautiously. "Of course you are. The Legion chose you for a reason, Keira. Maybe I . . . well I might have doubted it at first, I'll grant you. But I know you better now. And you are the most determined and hardworking person I think I've ever met. Maybe you don't see it, but you're leagues ahead of where you were when you got here."

Keira could feel a blush coloring her cheeks and glanced away from Danny's intent gaze.

"Keira, I don't pretend to understand who the Legion is or exactly what they have planned for us, but I do know people. And you deserve to be here. The Legion chose you because you have a part in this; we both do. This world may seem nice and bucolic, but Abalás is pretty removed from the goings-on in the rest of the country."

Danny took out his knife and began whittling away at a small wood block, a work in progress by the look of its scarred surface. He paused every once in a while to look up at her, gesticulating pointedly with the blade.

"Even here, we hear rumors. Bandits along the main throughways, rebels stirring up trouble . . . The Regio down in Crîd Eálas, he's old, Keira. He's old, and they say he's going senile. Meanwhile, his son has been away for years and has yet to be recalled from his studies in Mount Ánghen. The sages hold sway there, and they aren't about to give up the last remnant of some ancient tradition that has little place in today's world. But the people aren't happy. Their taxes are too high, raids along the coast too frequent, and sickness too rampant. The people are ready for a change."

"What's stopping them from getting it?" Keira asked. "Surely the government must know." She'd folded her legs underneath her and was leaning toward him, her interest piqued despite herself.

Danny snorted. "Empires aren't exactly known for their flexibility."

"Empires?" Keira asked. This was the first she was hearing of any empire.

"The Marian Empire—the most powerful force in this world a few hundred years ago. No one could stop their armies. Perfectly disciplined and absolutely lethal. But then, after only a few generations, they disappeared, their empire crumbling into dust and the leaderless factions left to fight over the remnant. Loren is one of the few countries left that still holds onto the heritage of its Marian conquerors, its Regios descended from the Marians themselves. Many compromises have had to be made over the years to preserve order in Loren. Meant to keep the people happy and the nobility placated, all they've really done is fray at the fragile ties holdin' this place together. It won't be long until those strands start to unravel, Keira. Anyone can see that. And it won't stop with Loren. This whole world will come apart. Chaos is looming, Keira. You can see it—in the animals, the trees, the people. The signs are everywhere. And the Legion, well, the Legion is here to stop it."

He paused, seeming to retreat somewhere inside of himself, before continuing on, "I've seen what war can do, Keira, the chaos it brings. I may not fully understand them, but if the Legion is trying to prevent that violence, well, that's something I can get behind."

Keira considered that for a long moment, finally nodding. "You have a point."

"Absolutely," he said.

Still, something made her pause. She glanced up as a sudden cold front blew the last remaining leaves from the trees overhead, sending a coarse shiver down her spine and a nervous edge that stung across her skin. Keira bit her lip. Was she really ready to commit to this shadowy, faceless organization? She knew basically nothing about it. It was a lot to ask, and possibly more than she was willing to give.

Keira's contemplative expression suddenly turned sour. Did it even matter? It's not like she had any other options. She looked at Danny and sighed. "I mean, I guess I have little choice, Danny. I'm here. And as far as I can tell, no one's about to help me get back to where I came from."

Danny nodded and gave her a considering look. "You're right, Keira. I don't know how to get back. I don't even know if that's possible. But . . . you have a choice." His eyes tightened, but he continued on, unabated. "You could find another life here. The Legion's not the only option. You have choices, and I want you to know that. I want you to feel like this path is one of *your* choosing. Otherwise, what's really the point? Sure, we can have order instead of chaos. But if it's forced upon us, it loses a lot of its appeal, don't you think?" He shrugged. "I may be just a dumb city kid from Boston, but if there's one thing I know, it's that the freedom to choose our own destiny is the most important thing, and it's something worth fighting for."

He paused, holding out his wood block for inspection in the filtered sunlight. "You have a choice, Keira. And whatever you choose, I'll do my best to help you get there."

Keira stared at him. "Why?" He looked confused and was about to answer when she continued, "You barely even know me, Danny. Why would you help me if I leave the Legion?"

Danny gave her a long, hard look. She stared back at him and could see thoughts churning behind his pale green eyes. He was clearly deciding what to say next, and she had the distinct impression that he was taking her measure, deciding how much to tell her.

"Keira," he began, "you and me, we're, well . . ." He scratched the back of his head, clearly seeking inspiration from among the surrounding trees.

"Has Elliott talked to you about binding yet, about pneuma? About how we're . . . connected?"

Keira's eyes widened and she stared blankly back at him, ignoring an entirely different type of shiver that coursed over her skin. He must have seen the shock on her face, for he quickly continued, "It's odd to say, I know, but . . ." He paused, glancing up at her, and came to some sort of conclusion in his head. "The midwinter festival is just a few weeks away, Keira."

She blinked. *That was some left turn*, she thought.

"Okaaay," she said. No idea where he was going with this.

"I'll talk to Elliott and Nazor, but, well, everything will be a lot easier to explain after the festival. So just don't decide yet, ok?" His eyes searched hers. "Just wait—wait until then."

Keira stared at him, feeling her own curiosity prickling under her skin.

"Ok," she murmured. "I'll wait until then."

He grinned at her, a look of relief crossing his face as he stood, brushing the dirt from his pants, and turned to go. As he neared the edge of the glade, he cast a parting word back at her. "And I'd grab some salve for those bruises. Elliott's got some in the cellar. Otherwise, you'll be in for a rude awakening tomorrow morning."

Keira groaned and flopped backward against the rocky bank. She stared up at the sky and wondered seriously whether she could actually make it through another week of this torture.

SEVENTEEN

The following weeks dragged on, each day harder than the one before. As Danny had predicted, Keira felt like she'd been run over by a truck and her mood wasn't much better. Nazor had zero pity for her and had them running through strenuous drills for hours on end, each day wearing Keira down a little more as she counted the days until she'd finally be free.

The morning of the winter solstice was crisp, and the horses' breath guided them as Keira and Danny turned their heads toward the road to town. Keira quickly urged Cerise into a trot, barely able to contain the grin that split across her face. She was *free*. As they rode into town, the noise of it struck her.

It had been over a month since their last visit to town and the sound of the market was overwhelming. The produce vendors of summer had been replaced by fur trappers hawking their wares and musicians playing to delighted crowds. Only the fishermen remained, their packed fish preserved even better in the subfreezing temperatures. Keira's excitement was tangible, and she felt more than saw Danny's eyes on her, no doubt amused by her excitement. She didn't care. She was off the farm, and there were people, real live, audible, touchable, smellable—and oh, did they smell—people.

Keira set off, Elliott's herb list in hand and Danny at her heels, trying to absorb the experience into her very pores. She marveled at the variety of sights, smells, and sounds that assaulted her senses. After an hour or so of browsing stalls and circulating among the crowds, Keira's nose was frozen and her toes were going numb. So, shopping items collected and her brain bordering on overload, she and Danny headed for the local tavern, called the Wailing Mudder.

Upon entering, she realized with a start that it was the same tavern she'd wandered into in search of a telephone on her first day in Loren. Looking about now, she decided it was largely unchanged, the air thick with Pandry smoke and a smorgasbord of tables filled almost to capacity.

All around her, the low murmur of excited spectators filled the air with anticipation. Keira grinned broadly at Danny and he couldn't help a small smile in return. Keira peered though the crowd, trying to catch the string of conversations that floated lazily through the air.

"—you heard? Troupe's come all the way from Port Galaén."

"Right posh if you ask me!"

"—well it *is* the midwinter festival!"

Then they passed a table of men, heads bent in shrouded conversation, brows furrowed and lips pressed into thin lines.

"New Bellators stationed along the fertile inlet—checking all the wagons headed to market."

"Skimmin' some off the top, no doubt."

"The Empire *will* have its cut."

"*Bastards.*"

"Steady on, they'll get what's comin' to them. Have no doubt."

Keira's eyes met Danny's in silent question and she saw a muscle flex in his jaw as he shook his head grimly, hurrying them past the men and their murderous mutterings.

Danny led her to a table at the far end of the tavern bordering a large, open space that occupied the center of the room. Keira collapsed into one chair with a dramatic flourish and a contented sigh. Danny snorted but merely raised one arm to summon a waiter. He took his seat and ordered hot drinks and food for them. Keira turned to survey the room, deciding that the space was indeed new and eagerly looked about for clues as to its purpose.

Their drinks arrived, and she readily wrapped her chilled hands around the steaming mug, inhaling deeply the spiced scent of mulled wine.

Danny laughed at her audible sigh. "I figured you'd prefer that to mudlo."

"What's mudlo?"

"Traditional uplander brew. Think whiskey but with a less pleasant afterburn."

Keira's eyes narrowed at the challenge and she leaned toward his proffered mug. But as the smell wafted toward her—something more akin to battery acid than any beverage she'd ever tasted—she curled her nose and shook her head.

"I think I'll stick with my wine, thanks."

Danny chuckled at her expression but merely shrugged and took a giant swig as he said, "Suit yourself."

Only in his gusto he drank too deeply and sputtered slightly as he cleared his windpipe. The sight was frankly comical and Keira's sharp peal of laughter startled them both. Danny grinned sheepishly back at her and she bit her lip to keep from laughing again. On a sudden impulse, she grabbed her own napkin and leaned across the table to dab at his chin.

"Here, you've got something . . ." Keira's voice trailed off as her eyes met his and she realized with a shock that their faces were only a few inches apart. Her eyes shot to his throat, which bobbed in an unsteady rhythm. Keira inhaled a sharp shaky breath before finishing, " . . . there."

She moved to sit back in her chair but Danny's hand moved lightning fast, catching hers and she froze, trapped as surely by those piercing green eyes as by any snare.

Her mouth suddenly felt dry and a not altogether unpleasant ache settled in her stomach.

"Keira . . ." Danny began, his voice surprisingly raw sounding.

"Yes?" She asked, trying desperately to ignore the hammering of her heart against her ribcage.

"There's something I—we—should have told you. The Legion, it's about more than just protecting order."

Keira blinked at him in confusion, not at all sure where he was suddenly going with this. But as he opened his mouth, presumably to continue, the lanterns suddenly dimmed, and the assembled crowd fell to a hush. His grip on her hand loosened and she slowly—not altogether willingly—settled back into her seat, ignoring how cold that hand suddenly felt. Shaking her head roughly, she turned toward the open space in the middle of the room.

As Keira's eyes adjusted to the lighting, she watched in astonishment as a beautiful woman, clothed all in white, entered center stage. As the lights dimmed, the circular edge of the space sputtered to life, the candles hurriedly lit by tavern attendants. The candlelight flickered off the woman's silver-white robes, and the strands of her alabaster hair seemed to ripple with its reflection. Keira hastily shut her mouth, as she realized it was hanging open, and watched in awe as the woman began spinning, weaving her torso around the edges of the circle as her dance filled the room with light. Without warning, Keira felt a warm presence beside her and she started as Danny's whispered words brushed against her neck.

"Some say she was the first of our kind, the first to seek order out of chaos, to control the pneuma."

She shivered despite herself before glancing to see that Danny had indeed shifted his seat to be right beside hers. Catching at her questioning look, he clarified, "Pneumos," and nodded to the spinning blur of white and silver in front of them. From the corners of the room, other dancers took to the stage dressed in flowing fabric of greens and blues. Keira stared in amazement as they moved to form mountains and flowing blue streamers made rivers that cut across the stage.

"Some say she existed before the universe itself, others that she was the first sentient being."

Beside her Danny shrugged. "I don't wade too deep into such questions myself."

Keira stared, enchanted by the way the dancer wove her arms, bending her body first one direction, then the other, her compatriots mimicking her motions as if shaped and moved by her very will. Keira could see the mountains forming and reaching toward the sky as rivers cut through the earth, separating land from water.

"But she was not alone. Another, called Séiro, sought to preserve the chaos, seeking power through the breaking rather than the building." At this, Danny gestured at another figure Keira hadn't noticed before, hooded in black and slinking along the ground at the edges of the light from Pneumos's lanterns. "It is said that they cannot exist apart, order and chaos, that things must be broken before they can be rebuilt into their truest form. But Séiro grew greedy, not wanting to share his power with Pneumos, and so undermined her efforts, breaking that which was good and corrupting its nature, until all was in a state of decay."

On the stage, Keira could see the dancer in black following in the footsteps of the spinning white blur, tapping the mountains and rivers so they crumpled to the ground, curling in on themselves.

"Seeing this danger, Pneumos created the spirit-binders, people that could harness her gift of pneuma and use it to shape matter from the void, creating order out of chaos."

Here Keira saw a man and woman, each richly ornamented in red-gold brocade, twined together in a twirling embrace.

Following in the wake of Séiro, the woman spun away from her partner, her leg coming up and over her head as she reached down to caress the crumpled mountains and rivers with a long, outstretched hand. Her other hand remained firmly grasped by the male dancer. He kept her rooted tightly, his face fierce as he shielded against some unseen foe.

"But Séiro refused to be thwarted so easily. He fought back against Pneumos, corrupting the hearts of her servants, who in their desperation to destroy him fed Séiro the very chaos he thrived on."

The hooded black figure had turned back to the golden couple by this point, and the three dove into a fierce battle of precisely timed martial arts that somehow looked more beautiful than lethal. While their battle continued, Pneumos came to kneel before the watching crowd, rocking side to side as her arms stretched out by her sides, and her face turned upward in a silent plea.

Keira was startled to see that the dancer herself was weeping openly, and she was not alone. Looking around the room, many of the audience had tears in their own eyes. She suddenly remembered her own pains, the silent hurts she carried around with her, the many tiny acts of destruction that had left the scars she felt now. She knew intuitively that everyone else in that room felt the same, that they reflected on the many wounds of their own lives. Keira wondered at the silence of the universe in the face of such pain.

The lanterns suddenly went out, and it cast the room into darkness. Expecting this, the crowd suddenly broke into applause as the lanterns were relit. Keira saw the dancers join hands and bow to the lauding crowd.

Startled, she turned to Danny, asking, "But how does it end?" He gave her a steady look, watching her reaction, and replied, "It doesn't. The fight goes on, order versus chaos, forever." She could tell he wasn't talking about the story anymore as he gazed into her face.

"The spirit binders," Keira breathed, eyes darting between the stage and Danny's all too serious affect. "That's—that's the Legion isn't it?"

Eyes fixed on her, Danny slowly nodded.

"We fight on, even though we know there will be no end. We fight for the world that might be. One in which order wins out over chaos and the building balances the breaking. All we can do is continue to fight and try to avoid taking the easier road, the one where we delude ourselves into thinking that pure destruction will lead to anything other than more destruction. We fight for what is right and along the way, try to build more than we break, to heal more than we destroy."

Keira stared at him, for the first time, truly seeing the path set before her. She inhaled sharply, a swirl of doubts filling her. There was no way she was up to the task.

"I don't know, Danny. I get that the Legion has this grand plan to bring order to the universe, but I still don't see how I fit in. How could I be any help in that?"

Danny's brow furrowed as he stared at her, before turning to gesture at the two red-gold dancers. "Keira," he began slowly, "*we* are the spirit-binders—you and me." Keira felt her eyes widen but Danny continued unabated.

"We're linked, just like them. Binding is what we were meant to do, Keira. It's why you're here. Swordsmanship, survival skills, that's all well and good. But *pneumonancy*, that is your true purpose."

Keira bit her lip as she looked between Danny and the dancers. She remembered the boiling water that Elliott had created, her intense curiosity about this seemingly impossible act. For a moment she thought of her mother, felt the familiar twinge of guilt. But for once, she pushed past it. Somehow, someway, she had to be a part of this. What that meant exactly, she wasn't sure. But there was one thing she did know—she wanted to learn pneumonancy.

She finally nodded.

"All right, Danny, I'll stay. But I want to learn spirit-binding. Not someday—now."

Danny exhaled through pursed lips, searching her face for something before finally nodding, eyes suddenly bright with excitement.

"Okay, we'll talk to Elliott and Nazor. I think it's time."

EIGHTEEN

Keira vomited, dry heaving up her empty stomach as she fell to her knees.

She felt Danny's warm hand on her back and let him help pull her to her feet. She accepted the cool glass of water that Elliott offered, returning his sympathetic smile with a glare.

"What the hell, Elliott? Why am I not getting this?"

Elliott sighed, arching one eyebrow. "It takes time, Keira. I warned you it wouldn't be easy. Our pneuma is unique to each one of us, residing deep within ourselves. To cast it outside of yourself, well, it can be a very jarring experience the first few times."

Keira gritted her teeth. There was an edge of sympathy in his voice that she found grating, even as she knew logically that it was well-intended. She did *not* like being coddled. She shoved the cup back to him and turned to Danny.

"Again," she said forcefully, squaring her shoulders and reaching out a hand toward him.

He looked hesitant. "Are you sure? We could always wait . . . try again tomorrow—"

"Now, Danny. We'll try it again."

He sighed. "Fine."

He reached out and grabbed her hand, squaring himself in his own grounding stance. His job was to pull her pneuma back to the ground —that is, if she could ever get it moving. Keira stared at the small pile of hay in front of her, alluringly flammable and yet so annoyingly unmoved.

You can do this, she told herself sternly. *You have to do this*. She may never be a brilliant swordsman, but this—she was born for this. Danny and Elliott had promised her as much.

She closed her eyes. Reaching deep within herself, just as Elliott had taught her, she searched for the pocket of energy she was determined to wrangle. In her mind's eye, she moved through every part of her body, nudging, feeling, waiting for inspiration to strike, waiting for the telltale sensation.

And there it was.

It was a small, pulsing ball of energy that lay just behind her stomach. She froze, holding her ground as she grew suddenly wary to touch it, her instinct clearly learning from prior experience. Luckily, her willpower was stronger than her instincts.

She nudged it, ever so gently, and felt it slowly uncoil. It grew larger, and she thrilled at the warmth she felt as it slithered out through her limbs, reaching the ends of her fingertips. It pulsed with a beat of its own that ran in syncopated rhythm with her own heartbeat. She tuned her mind's ear to that pulse, letting it fill her thoughts. Then, slowly, ever so gently, she whistled.

Nothing happened. The energy remained where it was, pulsing in her limbs as if not catching on. She tuned the pitch of her whistle, just slightly, and *there!*

Her pneuma leaped in recognition, clinging to the sound and forcing its way out of her. The energy pulse through her fingertips. She felt a swell of panic and firmly squashed it. Peeling open one eye and then the other, she tried her best to focus that energy on the small pile of hay and twigs. She ignored the blooming sensation of nausea, focusing instead in the direction she wanted her pneuma to flow.

And there it was. A small plume of smoke twisted and wound its way up from the hay. Excitement bloomed within her, even more powerful than the fear and nausea she was holding at bay.

She was doing it!

Her whistle became louder, almost unconsciously, as her excitement threatened to run away with her. The energy pulsed, a massive surge that burst its way out of her. She felt numb.

I'm going with it, she realized suddenly, as she felt herself being slowly peeled away from her body.

She panicked, clinging to her own body, trying to reel herself back in through her mind's eye.

Nothing.

She thought she heard a voice but couldn't make out the words. It was Danny. He was calling her name, calling her back. She struggled against the pull of the pneuma, desperately trying to untangle herself from its tentacled grip. But she was losing ground.

With every second she felt its pull strengthen as it dragged her inch by inch away from her body.

And then he was there.

Danny's pneuma was warmer than her own, its pulse faster and terrified.

She felt his pneuma latch onto her, felt it reel her back in.

Oh, thank God, she thought. *It's going to be ok.*

And then the memories came.

She was a small child, curled up in her bed as she listened to the screams and shouts from the kitchen below. She heard a dish breaking and she curled up tighter, trying to block out the sound of her mother's wail and the sobs that followed.

Then she was older, sitting at the dinner table with her mom, Tammy, and her latest boyfriend. She tried to ignore the boyfriend's leering smile, jerking her knee away from his probing fingers.

The scene shifted to the darkness of a bedroom she'd tried desperately to forget—to probing fingers, the fear and confusion of a violation she'd only later come to understand.

She squeezed her eyes tighter against the tears, willing the scene to disappear, for her to finally forget.

Please, please no. Not that, not now.

And then she was on the road, the winding road. Rain beat at the windshield as the car hit the guardrail, spinning and spinning out of control. It crashed through, and she felt the sickening sensation of her stomach dislodging as they sailed through the air.

She screamed.

She tried to wrench herself away from the foreign energy, the strange presence that made her relive her deepest, darkest secrets. She didn't want this. She couldn't bear it. Danny's voice grew louder.

"Keira! Keira, let me ground you!"

No. The moan was her own, silent in its plea.

"Hold on, let me help you."

"No!" she screamed. "I won't!"

And then there was a third presence, its pneuma cool and soothing, an aloe gel on her blistering, burned psyche. It wrapped itself around her, not daring to probe beneath the surface, merely guiding her, gently, back into herself.

Keira opened her eyes, looking straight into the warm gaze of Nazor, hands lightly cupped on either side of Keira's face.

Nazor's eyes were soft, not with sympathy but with understanding, acceptance. Keira breathed heavily, willing her heartbeat to slow. She flexed her fingers, reveling in their solidness.

"It's all right, child," Nazor murmured. "You're safe now. Nothing can hurt you."

Keira stared gratefully into those eyes, drinking in their surety, and willed herself to accept their promise. She searched their depths and saw only love and caring, without judgment or condemnation.

She nodded, taking a deep breath before climbing to her feet.

She turned and saw Danny, shifting his weight and rubbing a hand on the back of his neck as he stared apologetically at her. "Keira . . . I'm sorry. I didn't—"

"It's fine," she said, not bearing to fully meet his eye.

"I was trying to ground you, and—"

"It happens." Elliott's voice was soft and kind. "The relationship between cantor and grounder is complicated. A bind requires a level of intimacy that—"

"No." Keira's voice was firm.

"I'm sorry, I—"

"I won't do it." Keira's nausea had largely abated, leaving in its wake only utter exhaustion. "We're done, Elliott, done with all of this binding . . . stuff."

"Keira—"

"I'll stay," she said. "I'll learn sword fighting, archery, whatever else you want. But I'm done with binding. I'm not doing that again."

Elliott stared at her.

"Keira, pneumonancy is at the heart of what it means to be a Legionnaire. You can't just—"

"I can," Keira said, eyes narrowing. "I can, and I will."

"Keira—"

"Let her be." Nazor's interjection was firm, her eyes soft, but hands perched rigidly on her hips. "Leave the child alone, Elliott. It is her choice, what she chooses to share of herself. Let her be."

Keira shot Nazor a surprised look, shocked that she of all people should be on her side, but grateful nonetheless. Elliott and Nazor exchanged one of their patented indiscernible looks that spoke of an entire conversation happening behind the closed shutters of their eyes. Finally, Elliott nodded. "Very well, Keira. Why don't you head back to the house? Get some fresh air. We'll clean up here and join you for lunch shortly."

Keira nodded, even as the weight of shame brought with it the sting of tears. She fixed her eyes on the ground as she made her escape, knowing that a single sympathetic glance would be her undoing. Even so, she felt Danny's gaze on her. The horrified look she'd seen in his eyes told her everything she needed to know. He knew; he *knew*. Danny would never look at her the same way again—that much she knew—and she didn't think she could bear it.

CHAPTER

NINETEEN

Well *that* could have gone better.

Blowing hair out of his eyes, Danny roughly ran a hand across his forehead. His gaze followed Elliott and Nazor as they quietly gathered up the training materials from the barn's interior.

"Well?" He demanded, eyeing them both. "What do we do now?"

Nazor raised a single brow before rolling her eyes and turning to her black stallion. The horses had all been peering curiously from their stalls at their training session and now snorted with pleasure at her attention.

"Well, *I* for one, will be seeing to the horses. It's warmed up enough for a good turning out, don't you think?"

Frustration flared in Danny's chest and he shot his mentor a peevish look.

"I *meant* about Keira."

Nazor shrugged. "You heard her, she's finished. I don't see what else there is *to* be done."

Danny stared at her, dumbfounded. "You don't believe that. She—she's a cantor, my cantor. She can't just be *done*."

Nazor's gaze narrowed as she met his. "She has a choice, Danny. We all did. If this isn't what she wants, would you force her?"

"O-of course not!" Danny sputtered, eyes shooting to Elliott for some sort of assistance. But in Elliott he found only serene patience as he smiled kindly back at him. There was nothing more annoying than serenity when you felt like tearing your hair out.

"Give her time, Danny." Elliott said kindly. "She may come around, yet."

"And if we don't have time?"

Elliott's smile was grim as he patted Danny gently on the shoulder. "We're legionnaires, my boy. Nazor and I have a century at least between us. All we have is time."

"Well, good for you two," Danny grumbled. At their raised brows, he continued on. "You know as well as I do, we may not have time. Things are changing—even I can feel it. Rebellion, upheaval, it's coming. Sooner than we'd like. And without her, without Keira, what good am I? A grounder without a cantor. What use is that?"

Elliott gently squeezed Danny's shoulder. "You will find your way, both of you. Of that, I have no doubt."

Danny felt himself nodding even as his insides churned with wary indecision. Suddenly needing an escape, he made his excuses and hurried outside into the crisp midwinter air. He inhaled deeply, trying to cool the embers of his anger, but with little success. It was all well and good for Elliott and Nazor to talk of time. They had each other.

He'd lost everything at the end of a sniper's bullet—a family, a future, a life. Waking up in Loren and learning of the Legion and their mission, he knew this was his second chance, maybe the only chance he'd get to actually make something of his life. But it would all be for nothing if he couldn't convince Keira to stay. After all, what use was a grounder without a cantor to protect?

He would lose his chance, he would lose . . . *her.*

Her? When did this become about Keira herself? When did he stop seeing her as just his cantor and instead as his . . .what? Friend? Confidante? Something more?

And what exactly was it he'd seen in her memories when he'd tried to ground her just then? The picture had been hazy but the metallic tang of her fear had come through crystal clear. He wasn't the only one running from something. Could that be the actual source of her hesitation? Why she was suddenly so resistant to pneumonancy of any kind?

Danny buried his face in his hands, massaging his temples as if he could force the answers out himself. Glancing up, he saw a flash of movement through the kitchen window. Grim determination settled on him as his legs moved almost of their own accord, making for the cottage and the only person who could give him the answers he needed.

He found Keira in the kitchen, scrubbing roughly at the pewter cauldron with a wire brush and all the force of an avenging angel. Apparently, he wasn't the only one working through some things.

She must have heard him come in but she didn't look up from her work. Not sure where to start, he just stood there, leaning against the door frame as she took out her frustration on the cookware.

"Making progress?" He asked mildly.

"Let it go, Danny." Keira shot back, curt and dismissive in a way that made him clench his teeth.

He forced himself to relax and kept his voice innocent as he asked, "Let what go?"

"I'm not trying again."

"Not trying—?"

"Do *not* finish that sentence," Keira snapped, eyes finally meeting his in a show of defiance.

Danny clamped his mouth shut, fighting the pang of annoyance that surged through him. Pneumonancy was difficult, everyone knew that. Where the hell did she get off pretending she was so put upon?

"There's no need to just give up. We'll try again. You'll get it next time."

Keira snorted. "Ok, and what exactly will be different tomorrow?"

Danny groaned, "Well, with that attitude, nothing." He pinched the bridge of his nose, forcing himself to ignore the spark of defiance evident in her eyes. He sighed. "Come on Keira, you act as if you've never failed before."

"Of course I've failed," Keira snapped. But there was something about her voice and the coloring of her cheeks that made him pause and really look at her. Realization struck him.

"That's it, isn't it? You've never failed at anything." He might have laughed were it not for the furious glare Keira shot him. He quickly caught himself and forced his expression into one of serious consideration.

"Keira, everyone fails."

She stiffened at his words and even he winced at the unintended cord of condescension that wove through his words. "I just mean—"

She rolled her eyes so hard he was surprised she didn't pass out.

"Sure, Mr. *rides bareback and fights off bandits one-handed.* Oh yes, explorer of worlds and fighter of chaos, tell me more about how much you've failed."

Danny could only stare at her, dumbstruck. Was that really how she saw him? "Keira, I'm a grocer's kid who'd never left South Boston and barely graduated high school before being shipped off to war on another continent. And suddenly I've gotta not only survive, but keep other kids alive as well. You think I haven't *failed*?"

His words collided to a stop. He had zero desire to travel any further down that particular line of thinking—not today.

Keira stared back at him.

"Well, when you put it like that. . ." She gripped the edge of the counter as she leaned against it, kicking at the ground with a sheepish expression. "I—I guess it's more that I never got the chance to find out."

"Find out what?"

Keira sighed, a weary sound that echoed of wary fear and frayed resolve.

"I've failed plenty, Danny. It's just . . . I never know what happens after. Who's going to stick around? Who would want *me* around?"

Danny considered her for a long moment. She'd told him about her and her mother's living situation before. Shuttled from home to home, never more than a few months in any one place, of course Keira feared failure. She'd never gotten the chance to see who stuck around for the aftermath. For all she knew, failure left you alone without friend or future. To Keira, it was surely an endpoint, not a jumping off point.

He thought of his own failures, of the deep bonds of friendship that had carried him through, his fellow soldiers always ready with a clap on the back, a reassuring word, or just companionable silence. After all, they'd all been there. They all knew that particular brand of devastation well.

Danny smiled a small, sad smile. Coming to lean against the counter beside her, he gently nudged her shoulder with his own.

"You can't get rid of us that easily, Altman."

Her eyes met his and his breath caught in his throat. Their sapphire blue depths shone back at him, cut through by the dagger-like edge of hope. He couldn't breathe, didn't want to breath. *Pneumos*, but he could get lost in those eyes.

All too quickly, she looked away and Danny seized on the reprieve to quiet the thudding of his own heart. Seriously, what was *wrong* with him?

"Even if . . ." Keira paused, clearly fighting to keep some powerful emotion from bubbling to the surface. "Even if there's some truth to what you're saying, Danny, it changes nothing. I'm done with pneumonancy. It's not just that I can't, it's that, I . . . I don't like it."

Danny's brows furrowed as Keira glanced furtively at him and then away, fingers twisting at the edges of her tunic in a way that was decidedly *un*-Keira like. Then a thought occurred to him.

"Keira, this isn't about what I saw, is it? With your Mom? And—and her boyfriend?"

Keira's eyes widened slightly and all the blood seemed to drain from her face. Danny moved to step toward her but she stumbled backward and he froze, feeling suddenly adrift with no idea what to do.

"You shouldn't have seen that," Keira whispered. "It—it wasn't yours to *see*."

"I—I'm sorry Keira. I should have warned you. The bond—grounders, we can sense things through the bond, thoughts, emotions, memories even."

Keira's pale skin turned a shade of green around the edges and she let out a guttural sound that made the hair stand up on Danny's neck. "That's what I was afraid of."

Danny stared at her, trying to calm the racing thoughts that left him muddled and off-kilter. But one thought stood above the rest, one memory. The slimy feel of fingers on her leg and the rattle of a bedroom door in the night, the crippling fear that left her frozen as the amorphous figure creeped steadily toward her.

And then Danny went still, utterly, terrifyingly still.

"Keira, what *was* that?"

Keira stiffened at his words before rising to the entirety of her five feet and two inches. Her chin lifted defiantly as she held his gaze. "You know what it was."

There was a roaring in his ears as Danny just stared at her, his brain trying desperately to process the icy truth already creeping through his body. At a loss, he choked out, "Why didn't you tell anyone?"

Keira gaped at him, shock and hurt warring across her features. He knew his words were callous but he didn't have time to backtrack before she whispered, "I did, Danny. I *did*."

He felt sick. His fingernails cut into his palm and he realized with a jolt that he was shaking, whether from nausea or fury, he couldn't say.

"Tell me that bastard's in prison at least."

Keira seemed to swallow convulsively, her eyes shining with

unshed tears. She shook her head once . . . twice, brisk staccato movements that were tight and controlled, giving Danny the distinct sense that one wayward millimeter would leave her unraveled entirely.

"Why the hell not?" He growled.

Keira's mouth opened and closed, her eyes darting from side to side like a cornered animal. Vaguely some better part of himself registered her distress, could see her desperation for escape. But he was too busy wrestling his own anger into place, trying to still the shaking in his own body. So he just stood there, letting her squirm, his presence demanding an answer she clearly didn't want to give.

The seconds dragged on, each one adding a weight that bore down on them as they each stood their ground, building and building until something had to crack.

"Keira—"

"Because she didn't believe me!"

Danny blinked, opened his mouth, but Keira wasn't done.

"Well? Is that what you want to hear? My own mother didn't believe me, chose *him* over me. Not that it mattered." She choked out a strangled laugh devoid of all humor. "He was out of our lives only not two weeks later. Seems he didn't feel inclined to return the sentiment. Still . . . she chose him."

Danny stared at her, understanding finally dawning, closely followed by a fury unlike any he'd ever known. It coursed through him, leaving behind a searing pain like freshly burned skin. He felt his fists clench and for the first time in his life felt truly murderous—it was terrifying.

He fought for control, knowing that what Keira needed just then certainly wasn't his righteous indignation.

"Then why on earth would you want to go back?" The words came out choppy, his barely contained rage making each syllable a crisp staccato. "She doesn't deserve a daughter like you. Not after what she did."

Keira stared at him, incomprehension clear on her face.

"Because she needs me." She said the words as if they were the most obvious in the world. And Danny knew she'd internalized them to her very core.

"You can't be serious."

"What, you think she can take care of herself? She couldn't even protect her own daughter. She's *my* responsibility, *mine* to protect."

"And what about you? Didn't you deserve protection? I think she gave up any right to your sympathies that night when she—"

"Stop," Keira snarled. "I wouldn't expect *you* to understand."

That caught him up short and his eyes narrowed on her, all the anger he felt at an absent party finding someone closer to home to target.

"What the hell is that supposed to mean?"

"Nothing."

"No, please, Keira." Danny insisted, voice laced with sarcasm. "Explain yourself."

Keira's eyes narrowed. "I don't have to explain anything to you. I don't *owe* you anything."

Danny barked a harsh laugh. "Really? I don't see anyone else around trying to keep you from getting yourself killed. If not me, who? Nazor? Elliott? I haven't seen any thank-you notes headed *their* way lately."

"Bastard."

"Lovely as usual."

Keira shook her head, disgusted, before pushing off from the counter. "You know what? I don't have to take this, not from you. I'm done." He opened his mouth to reply but she beat him to it. "Not just with pneumonancy, Danny, with all of it. I think it's past time I left."

Danny gaped at her. "And where exactly do you think you're going to go?"

"No idea," she snapped. "And I don't really care. Just so long as it's far away from *here*."

Something sank in the pit of his stomach at her words, but he shoved the feeling aside, too furious to deal with anything else. She moved toward the staircase and he quickly cut her off, folding his arms over his chest and leveling her with a glare.

"Yeah? Well, what's the plan, Keira? Just going to run off? It's almost dusk. You'll freeze."

"I'm not an idiot, Danny, no matter what people around here seem to think. I'll leave in the morning. I don't know where. Maybe the village, maybe the city. Someone in this world has to know a way home. And if you all won't help, I'll find someone who will."

He rolled his eyes at her dramatic declaration, feeling more than a little satisfaction at her seething glare. She made to shove past him and he let her pass. But at the last moment, he snagged her arm. Her head whipped around toward him.

"Let me—"

"One more thing, Keira. If you do somehow find a way back, you really should tell your mom to screw off." Danny took a deep breath, willing himself to calm down. "You may not see it now. But one day, you'll realize you don't owe her anything. That who you are, who you want to be. That's up to you. You are who you are despite your mother, not because of her."

Keira swallowed, the muscle in her jaw clenching and unclenching.

"Is that all?"

Something heavy sunk into the pit of his stomach. But he let go of her arm.

"Yeah, that's all."

Without another look back at him, she climbed the stairs. And with a hollow feeling, he watched as she slipped away.

CHAPTER
TWENTY

Keira slung the saddle bag across one shoulder as she slipped out the door of her bedroom. She spared one last glance at the bare room that had been her home for the last few months before shutting the door with a decisive click.

It was time to go. Beyond time, actually. Keira had fled to her room after the argument with Danny before promptly bursting into tears. She'd stayed there through dinner, unable to get control of herself and unwilling for the others to see her that way. Most of the night she'd laid awake, rehashing the day and the argument until she was left with only one conclusion.

She really had to leave.

She'd always intended to, she reminded herself. She'd only agreed to stay so she could train and learn how to stay alive in this new world. The plan had always been to find a way home. Guilt had clawed at her then, as she remembered her too long neglected goal. How had she allowed herself to become so distracted? To become so caught up with sword fighting and magic wielding that she'd forgotten the most important thing. Her mom needed her, might even be in danger. No, it was time to leave—past time actually.

These were the thoughts racing through her head as Keira softly padded through the cottage, making her way toward the front door.

"I suppose it's true then."

Keira started at the unexpected voice and spun to see Nazor perched at the table, nursing a steaming mug between both hands.

Keira straightened herself to her full, albeit unimpressive height and looked Nazor directly in the eye.

"It's time I was going, Nazor."

Nazor arched a single brow. "Oh is it, now? Just part of the plan, then. Nothing at all to do with yesterday, I suppose."

Keira's stomach flipped but she didn't flinch. She was done letting Nazor intimidate her.

"Yesterday was just a reminder. I don't belong here, Nazor. I never have. It's time I focused on finding a way home."

"To your mother."

Nazor said the words bluntly, without question.

"Yes, my mother." Keira said sharply. Then she sighed. "I can't just give up on finding her, on going home. It just wouldn't—"

Keira sighed, shaking her head roughly as she switched the shoulder strap to the other side. "You wouldn't understand."

Nazor tilted her head, considering, her eyes a dark pool lined with sharp edges.

"I understand better than you think."

Keira raised her brows.

"Your life was never your own, Keira. It was always defined by others. Their hopes, their fears, their desire for who you might be . . . to *them*."

Keira swallowed, forcing her expression to remain blank, unwilling to yield an inch of understanding for the woman who'd made her life miserable these past few weeks.

"I know what that's like, what the weight of that expectation can do to a person. But I ask you to consider who you might have been. Who might you have become if freed from tragedy? If released from the weight of *her* choices?"

Keira's breath caught in her throat and she swallowed convulsively.

"I know who I am, Nazor. And I know what I want. I want to go home and I will find a way, whatever it takes."

Nazor's lips pursed as she considered Keira, her usually unreadable expression torn. Then she blinked and her enigmatic smile slid effortlessly back into place. She nodded briskly.

"At least take this."

Keira blinked in surprise as Nazor passed her a large carefully wrapped bundle. With unsteady fingers, Keira unwrapped it to find packages of food and preserves. Something warm filled Keira's chest as her eyes darted up to meet those of her most stoic, unfeeling mentor.

Nazor shrugged, one hand rubbing against the back of her neck.

"You missed dinner," she said gruffly. "No sense starving."

Keira blinked against the sting of tears that suddenly pricked at her eyes as she tore her gaze away and back down to the bundle of carefully arranged food. Far more than a single dinner's worth, she thought wryly.

Unable to muster words of thanks, Keira merely nodded and carefully placed the food in one of her saddle bags.

For her part, Nazor seemed relieved to have avoided an emotional scene. She stood as Keira moved toward the door.

"Where will you go?"

"Abalás," Keira said. "At least at first. Then to Port Galaén, to track down the Legion and their supposed library. After that . . ." She let her words trail off as she shrugged.

"I hope you find what you're looking for, Keira." Nazor said quietly. "But if not, know you always have a place here."

Keira swallowed convulsively as she stood in the doorway, before finally managing. "Thank you, Nazor."

And then she left. Hearing the door rumble to a close behind her, it clicked with an ominous thud. Keira strode quickly to the stable to ready Cerise. Now that she really was leaving, she wanted nothing more than to get as far away as possible.

"Time to go, girl." She whispered into Cerise's flaxen mane. The mare nuzzled her in response and Keira inhaled deeply, steadying herself before swinging into the saddle. She guided Cerise along the trail leading to the main road, every step bringing with it a strange sense of both excitement and nerves. She was really doing it, finally striking out on her own.

Yet reaching the main road, she hesitated. To the right lead into Abalás, where a warm tavern promised a place to plan her next move. But to the left . . .

Keira inhaled deeply the crisp morning air of midwinter. To the left lay the riverbank where she'd first arrived in Loren. How many times had she walked its length, praying for some sign, some way back home? Not for several months, the guilty voice in the back of her mind reminded her. She'd been too busy learning sword fighting and pneumonancy. Too busy building a life where she had no business being.

Almost unconsciously, Keira steered Cerise to the left. She had to see, just one more time, if there was any way back. She knew it was foolish, knew that wasn't how pneumonancy worked. Even so, she had to try . . . one last time.

CHAPTER

TWENTY-ONE

Danny barely slept the entire night, rehashing over and over the argument with Keira. Just when he'd begin to drift off to sleep, some infuriating detail of the conversation would pop into his head and he'd let the frustration course through him all over again.

Who the hell did she think she was?

They'd all been bending over backward to help her train, to teach her everything she needed to know to survive, to become a legionnaire. And all for what?

So she could be done? Just like that?

He hadn't taken her for a quitter. But hey, what did he know?

He clung to the anger that coursed through him, needed it. Because as soon as it began to fade, he was left with nothing but a seemingly endless well of despair. How long had he waited for his Cantor to arrive? How long had he bid his time, waiting for his person, the missing half his pneuma had so yearned for?

Well, he'd found her alright, and she'd been nothing like what he expected.

Keira was stubborn, headstrong, and convinced beyond reason that she was right. It was infuriating; *she* was infuriating.

And Pneumos did he miss her.

He froze, the thought hanging in the air like some ominous specter.

He *missed* her? She wasn't even gone yet. How could he *miss* her?

He'd been so convinced when she'd arrived that there'd been some mistake, that she couldn't possibly be the Cantor he'd been waiting for. And now here he was, *missing* her?

He sighed, flipping first onto his stomach and then onto his back. Finally deciding there was nothing for it, he sat up abruptly and began yanking his boots on. Sleep obviously wouldn't be finding him, and besides, it was almost dawn anyway. Might as well get to work and try to figure out what in the blazes he was going to say to Keira when he saw her.

Danny thudded down the stairs, half hoping she'd be there already, no doubt still furious with him, but both equally chagrined of their childish behavior.

Instead, there was only Nazor and Elliott, both eating their breakfast in somber silence.

Danny swallowed, letting the despair wash over him once more. She couldn't — she couldn't actually have *left*, could she? But one glance at their faces confirmed the worst.

She was really gone.

He blinked, gritting his teeth before striding toward the kitchen and the steaming pot of porridge still simmering over the fire.

He took his seat across from Nazor and Elliott without a word, staring instead at his bowl as he roughly shoveled the contents into his mouth.

"She left about an hour ago," Elliott said carefully, eying Danny for his reaction. "Nazor saw her off."

Danny merely grunted in response and from the corner of his eye saw Elliott and Nazor exchange inscrutable glances.

"She took the road into town." Nazor murmured. "I expect she'll hole up at the local tavern while she figures out her next move."

"Well, good for her."

The words came out more bitterly than he'd intended and he ignored the raised brow look that passed between Nazor and Elliott.

"She's your cantor, Danny," Elliott said gently. "If anyone could get through to her, it's you."

Danny snorted.

"Have you met her?"

"Keira can be stubborn, I know, but she's running scared Danny."

Danny rolled his eyes.

"Scared? Stubborn as hell is more like it."

Elliott pressed his mouth into a thin line, and Danny assiduously avoided his disapproving gaze. Elliott would *not* make him feel guilty. Not for this. Keira had made her choice, not him.

"You know how important this all is," Elliott pressed. "Without a cantor, you cannot hope to—"

"Look, I was doing just fine on my own." Danny snapped. "Something tells me the Legion will still find some use for me, even without a cantor."

Nazor snorted loudly.

Danny rounded on her, eyes sparking.

"What?"

"That's rubbish, and you know it."

Danny narrowed his eyes at his mentor.

"Danny," Nazor's voice dropped to a low rumble. "For as long as I've known you, you've longed for nothing more than partnership, for the one person you can trust implicitly. You were searching in your old life and you're still searching now."

Danny opened his mouth to argue, cheeks burning, but Nazor wasn't through.

"What you *lack* is empathy, my boy. The understanding that the world as you see it is not necessarily the same for Keira. And until you can see the situation from her perspective, and convince *her* of that, you two will never be as one, not really."

Danny gritted his teeth, remembering the snarled words of their last argument.

"Yeah, well, maybe she's just not the right partner, Nazor. Ever think of that?"

Nazor raised one brow and leveled him with an incredulous look.

"You don't really believe that, Danny. If you did, you wouldn't be hurting so much."

Elliott reached out then and squeezed Danny's shoulder in condolence.

"She's your cantor, Danny. You know it, we know it, and deep down, so does she. You are pneuma-bound and there is nothing stronger than that bond. Nothing."

Danny swallowed, remembering the weeks spent training together, exploring Abalás, or tramping through the forest looking for some herb Elliott needed for his poultices. He remembered her too-loud laugh that came straight from her belly. The way her entire face scrunched up when she was concentrating. The wide-eyed, incredulous look she'd shot him the first time she felt her pneuma and realized the possibilities of her own power.

They were right.

Infuriating though she may be, there was an invisible thread that bound them, an inexplicable connection that he couldn't possibly articulate but felt as strongly as ever. Pneuma-bound. Cantor and grounder. Forever linked.

Danny swallowed, looking between the knowing gazes of his mentors. He shook his head.

"It—it's too late. She's gone."

The sense of despair he felt at his own words snatched the breath from his lungs. How could he have been so blind?

"She'll have made for the village," Nazor remarked quietly. "To regroup."

Elliott grinned broadly, clapping him on the shoulder even as Danny, snatched his overcoat from the hook by the door.

"Give her our best, won't you?"

Danny barely had time to nod before he barreled out the door, making for the stable at a dead sprint. If he hurried, maybe he could catch her before she reached the village. Though what he'd say when he did was anyone's guess. But somehow, some way, he'd make her see.

CHAPTER

TWENTY-TWO

The dewy promise of the morning quickly turned to an ominous gray as Keira guided Cerise along the path to the riverbank. Thick cloud cover obscured any view of the sun and there was an electric buzz in the air that made the hair on her neck stand on end.

Keira reigned Cerise to a stop as the path once again forked into three.

She bit her lip.

She'd traveled this way a few times with Danny, heading to the riverbank for some lesson in fishing or navigation, but she'd never traveled it on her own. And she certainly didn't recall there being so many options.

Sensing a gradual decline in the slope of the land, Keira urged Cerise to the left, praying that this way really did lead down to the riverbank and the first place she'd arrived in Loren.

The wind picked up even as the tree cover somehow grew thicker. Surely they had to be close now. Wasn't—

A streak of lightning pierced the air, followed swiftly by a crack of thunder and Cerise reared. Keira fumbled for the reins, thighs clenched as she desperately fought to keep her seat.

But it was too late.

Keira landed hard, directly on her tailbone.

Stunned but clinging to her last shreds of wherewithal, Keira rolled out of the way of Cerise's flailing hooves, just before they thudded back to earth—missing her head by inches.

As soon as her hooves hit the ground, Cerise was off at a dead gallop, headed no doubt back to the farmhouse and the warm stall that awaited her.

Barely catching her breath, Keira rolled and stumbled to her feet, calling out in despair for Cerise even as the rumble of her hooves echoed far off into the distance.

Fear unlike any she'd ever experienced tightened viselike around her chest.

Keira felt her legs give way as she slowly sank to the ground.

That had been close, too close.

What a fool she'd been, thinking she could go off on her own like this. Had she learned nothing?

Typical Keira, reliant on no one and nothing. Well, look what that had gotten her now.

An unfamiliar ache settled between her ribs, a longing for place that she barely recognized.

Oh, what she'd give to be back in that old farmhouse, laughing with Danny and Elliott, Nazor looking on disapprovingly but secretly enjoying their delight.

Keira's eyes stung and she blinked away the traitorous tears. She'd made her bed. She knew better than to cry over it.

A loud crack echoed through the night.

Keira froze.

That was not thunder.

Her breath came in stinging gulps as her eyes darted between the dark shadows of the treetops. Their twisting boughs were a wicked complement to the knotted roots that jutted out from the ground, intent on catching her unawares.

She didn't belong here.

Another crack sounded from not far behind her and she spun, heart hammering in her chest. She backed away only to stumble, landing in a heap of limbs against a nearby boulder.

All she wanted in that moment was to curl in on herself, to hide her face and pretend that all was well, but a familiar growl echoed in her ears.

Oya, little Keira. You know better than to huddle in fear. You will face death when it comes for you.

At Nazor's words, Keira forced her shaky limbs into submission and stumbled to her feet, gripping the boulder for support.

She may not belong in this world but by God she was not the same meek, scared girl who'd first arrived—too afraid of her own abilities to stand out, to step forward, to be truly *seen*.

No, she was not that girl any longer.

So as the rustling in the bushes grew louder, Keira slowly drew her sword, letting the ring of steel echo through the night.

Her eyes held wide open to the danger that loomed ahead.

~

"What do you mean, she's not here?"

Danny fought to keep his temper in check as the beady eyed barkeep shrugged indifferently. When the storm hit, it had forced him to seek shelter in the tavern along with a crowd of other travelers. But he hadn't been able to corner the bustling owner until now. Even so, he had the distinct impression he wasn't getting the man's full attention as he scanned the small crowd with an eager and overly solicitous smile.

"No one 'ere by that description. I'd remember a young lass like that, don't you think?"

The barkeep shot him a wink, followed by a leering grin and Danny felt his nails bite painfully into his palms.

Don't hit him. Don't hit him.

Since starting a tavern brawl would lend nothing to his search, Danny contented himself with a glare that immediately sent the man scurrying into the back.

Danny dragged a hand across his face as he racked his brain.

Where else could she have gone?

He'd already confronted each of the other travelers in the tavern to see if they'd spied a young woman traveling alone on the road and their looks of alarm and hasty assurances that *that* sort of thing would have caught their attention did nothing to ease his nerves.

He glanced toward the window and noted with satisfaction that the rain had slowed to a drizzle.

So, after one last glance around, Danny shoved his way back out through the tavern doors, letting them slam together with a satisfying thud.

Where *was* she?

As he mounted Boyd and steered him back toward the farm, Danny let his frustration bubble to the surface, anything to ignore the rising fear threatening to take its place.

Maybe she'd turned back, come to her senses about this whole ridiculous thing, and realized her home was with them—with *him*.

He swallowed, trying to squelch the bloom of hope that sparked in his chest. He just needed to find her. Once he did . . . well, then everything else would make sense.

It had to.

Danny kneed Boyd into a trot and it didn't take long before they reached the turnoff from the main road that led to the farm.

And that was when he saw it.

Breath fled from his lungs as a crushing pressure filled his chest. He stared in horror at the riderless mare with flaxen mane grazing just off to the side of the road.

Cerise.

Full-blown panic ripped through him and Danny nearly broke his neck, straining to see any sign of Keira nearby.

But of course, there was nothing.

He leaped from the saddle and hurried toward the horse, taking care not to spook her as he neared. He quickly scanned her for any sign of injury.

"What happened, honey." He whispered, stroking her nose as she nuzzled his chest in greeting.

His eyes flicked across the road for any sign of—

There.

Danny led Cerise by the reins as he kneeled to examine the barest hint of tracks leading along the road, away from both Abalás and the farm. They were faint, barely visible after the storm, but Danny was sure that was the direction Cerise had come from.

Fury once more bloomed in his chest.

How could Keira have been so stupid? Heading out on the open road right before a storm? Without supplies? Without a plan? How could she—and then he froze, realization suddenly dawning on him.

"The river," he breathed, trying to squelch the dread sending waves of nausea coursing through him. "She went to the river."

The river.

With its silty banks that easily flooded given the mildest conditions and the raging storm that had just passed . . .

Danny shoved the thought from his mind, forcing himself to focus on the practical. He quickly lashed Cerise's reins to Boyd's saddle and sprung into it himself, urging them forward to the fastest trot he dared in the muddy road. He kept all his attention focused on the road ahead and refused to think about what might have happened.

He just hoped he wasn't too late.

TWENTY-THREE

Keira wasn't sure when she started running. But she sure as hell wasn't planning to stop.

With each step, her feet sunk deeper into the muddy ground. She tried to look behind her as she ran, ignoring the sharp sting of branches as they hit her face.

Her foot caught on a gnarled root and she stumbled, grimacing as her knee jarred painfully into a nearby rock. She tried to ignore the leering chuckles that echoed from behind her as she stumbled back to her feet and kept running. She shoved aside a wall of branches and barreled through, blinking in surprise as she emerged in a moonlit clearing of trees before an enormous rock face. Keira gaped in surprise as she stared up at the massive outcropping that materialized from the forest floor. Where had it come from?

The sound of crunching footsteps brought her back to reality as she spun in alarm to face the wall of trees. Her eyes darted to either side but the moss covered rock face cut inward in a curving line from either side of her position.

She was trapped.

Hand trembling, Keira unsheathed the sword at her hip and moved into a guard position. She tried to slow her breathing, remembering everything Nazor had taught her as her eyes fixed on the tree line.

"Right foot forward . . . Bend your knees! . . . Are you at ease or at the ready?"

She could practically hear the warrior woman barking in her ear and the thought was oddly soothing, as if she weren't as completely alone as she felt in that moment.

Then the first leering face emerged from the darkness.

Keira tightened her grip on her sword and settled into her stance. Then another . . . and another . . . and another. Keira tried to fight the buoy of panic as five or six grown men emerged from the tree line, all chuckling and leering at her, each armed with an axe or club.

Keira tried to keep her breathing even as they slowly encircled her.

Then she snapped.

She lunged forward, sword flashing but the men in front of her merely stepped back, batting her blade away, even as the men to the side surged forward. Keira spun, trying and failing to keep them all in sight.

A leg flashed in her peripheral vision and suddenly her feet were swept out from under her.

She cried out as she caught herself against the rock face.

The men chuckled in a low, throaty rumble that sent ice down Keira's spine. She struggled to stay upright, forcing herself to breathe deeply as they encircled her.

Do not freeze, Altman. Don't you dare freeze.

But already she could feel the edges of her vision darkening as the weight of memory washed over her.

This is not then. This is now. I am here, not there.

She recited the words like a chant in her mind, willing herself to stay upright. If this was the end, then by god she wasn't going to go quietly.

And that's when she felt it.

The nudge of energy in her belly, prodding her, pleading even, to be let loose.

It took only a moment's hesitation, a moment's pause, before she seized upon it, letting the pneuma flood through her limbs.

She had no plan, no aim. There was only her own desperation and the pneuma that promised some chance of escape.

Kneeling to the ground, she pressed her fingertips into the moist earth and focused all her attention on the patch of grass before her. She imagined it breaking apart into glorious chaos and on the back of an unheard whistle sent her intention flying through the air.

The spot erupted into flames.

She gaped at it in surprise.

"I—I did it," she whispered, feeling a surge of satisfaction as the bandits stumbled back with shouts of alarm. The flames weren't high —no more than two or three feet, but their sudden inexplicable appearance on the damp riverbank was enough to cause shouts of alarm.

Keira focused on expanding the spot, slowly curling the wall of flames into a circle around herself.

But it was slow going and she could feel herself weakening.

Just hold on, she begged. *Just a little longer.*

"Bleedin' witch!"

Keira's eyes darted up just in time to see a meaty fist strike the side of her face.

The ground rushed towards her, and she collided with a bone-jarring thud. Keira struggled to breathe as loud guffaws of laughter echoed around the clearing.

The flames crackled angrily but she could barely hear them above the ringing in her ears. With trembling hands, she braced herself against the ground, preparing to stagger to her feet. But a hand gripped the nape of her neck and dragged her to standing. She cried out, but her words were whipped away from her by the howl of wind and the chortles of men.

"Lot o' trouble you've put us through missie."

Keira inhaled the scent of burned grass and unwashed human flesh, nearly gagging at the onslaught. Her eyes darted across the ground.

My sword, where's my—

She spotted it lying unnoticed to the right and lunged for it. But the fist tightened around her collar and she choked, swinging wildly with her fists while the men laughed in amusement. Tears sprung to her eyes, blurring the picture in front of her as despair, so far held at bay, swelled within her.

This is it, she thought.

Her second chance at life was about to be snuffed out with one reckless decision.

If only—

A sharp whistle coursed through the air and the brigand's harsh laugh was replaced by wet gurgles. Keira glanced up in alarm to find a single arrow jutting angrily from the man's throat.

Slowly, inexorably, she turned in the direction it had come from.

And there he was.

"Danny," her voice cracked on the word. But she didn't try to fight the swell of relief that surged through her. There he was, at the edge of the clearing, bow raised, green eyes flashing, and looking absolutely murderous.

"Take. Your. Hands. Off. Her."

She gaped at him for just a moment before feeling the brigand's grip loosen on her collar. Seizing on his distraction, she elbowed him in the throat and was rewarded with a spluttering moan.

His hand slipped away and she once more lunged for her sword, spinning just in time to block the downward swing of another man's hatchet. She heaved the weapon to the side and brought her leg up to kick him squarely in the gut.

He stumbled back.

Seizing the opportunity, she lunged forward.

A hand circling her wrist caught her short and she spun, bringing her sword up and around.

Danny caught her other hand just before she sliced into him.

Keira gaped in surprise.

"How—"

"Not now, sweetheart. I'm a tad—,"

Danny spun, pulling her behind him as he blocked an overhead swing from a club wielding behemoth of a man.

"—busy."

"I'm not your—"

Keira cut herself off with the shake of the head. This was *sooo* not the time.

"I see you've reconsidered the whole no-pneumonancy thing." Danny grunted as he slashed at one of the men, before shoulder checking a second away from her. "Nicely done."

Keira blinked at him, ignoring the warm flush of pleasure at the compliment. Then she scowled.

"Yeah, well fat lot of good it did me."

She lunged forward, arcing her sword wide as two of the remaining brigands tried to sneak up their flank. They were fighting shoulder to shoulder now, the earlier flames long since settled down into a low simmer.

"I don't know. Seemed a good start to me. Only you need to go a bit . . . bigger."

Danny held his hand out to her then and Keira blinked at it— knowing in an instant exactly what he was asking. Going bigger meant casting out a lot farther. Something she could only do with, yep . . . a *grounder*.

Keira eyed the advancing brigands nervously. They were still outnumbered. Even with Danny by her side, well, even he had his limits.

"It's your choice, Keira."

Keira glanced up to see Danny's green eyes fixed on her, and for a moment, she couldn't breathe.

"Always," he whispered.

The moment was cut short by the curse of a short, stout man who lunged toward Danny—spear aimed directly at his chest.

Danny dodged out of the way, shoving Keira to the side so that the spear cut just between them. Danny snatched its shaft, his sword coming down on the wood so it shattered into two. His face was one of pure fury as he flipped the spear in his grip and sent it shooting through the air—directly at the stout man's chest.

"You wanna try me?" Danny snarled, pointing his sword at each of the remaining men. "Huh?"

Keira couldn't help but marvel at him. This boy she barely knew, willing to risk his own life—for her. And in that instant, she knew that whatever came next—she could trust him.

He would never leave her.

Never abandon her.

And as Keira knew better than anyone, that was no small thing.

Her breath caught as the men regarded each other, then calmly advanced—slowly but steadily penning the two of them in.

It was now or never.

With a sharp inhale, Keira seized onto Danny's hand before she could think better of it.

The pneuma inside her was already uncurled, at the ready for just this moment. Keira focused on it, dimly aware of Danny tugging her body behind him even as his pneuma wrapped around hers. Lightly, gently, but ever securely tethering her into place. With a jolt of surprise, Keira realized that it actually felt . . . good.

Instead of pinned down, she felt . . . anchored. And with that steady assurance, she let her pneuma surge forward and she right along with it.

In an instant, she wasn't just seeing the grass. She *was* the grass. Every molecule buzzing, she sent her pneuma to fill the in-between places, letting it expand until the molecules themselves melted away and the grass became something other, something *more*.

She became aware of herself first by the rush of heat that assaulted her front, then by Danny's frantic shouts.

"Keira! Keira! You did it, come back!"

She slammed back into her body with a force that sent her staggering backwards.

And there was Danny.

His face was a mix of emotions—fear, concern, and yes, *pride*. And he was haloed by . . . hang on a second.

Flames.

His face was surrounded by flames.

And then there was only darkness.

TWENTY-FOUR

The first thing Keira was aware of as she came to was the feel of a warm, calloused hand on her cheek, and the scent of ashes in the air.

As her eyes fluttered open, the first thing she saw was Danny's face, a floating mixture of awe and concern that hovered just above her head.

"You all right?"

She sat bolt upright.

Eyes scanned the dark clearing, now lit only by the full moon—searching for flames, for bandits, for *something*.

"Where'd they go?" Keira demanded, rounding on Danny.

He sat crouched in the dirt before her, wiping the bloody steel of his blade against the still-moist grass.

"Gone," he said simply, shrugging. "Ran off at the first site of that flame wall. Well timed, by the way." He quirked a grin at her that made Keira's stomach flip-flop. But her brow furrowed at his words.

"Flame wall?"

"Yeah, ten feet easy and curled perfectly around us. Don't think Elliott could've done better himself."

Keira exhaled heavily but bit her lip as another thought suddenly occurred to her.

"Did I—" Keira swallowed, suddenly self-conscious of her question but unable to look away. The rest came out in a raw whisper. "Did I kill anyone?"

Danny's face softened as he took in her anxious expression. He shook his head.

"Naw, leave it to men like that to have an excellent sense of self-preservation. Your hands are clean, sweetheart."

Keira sighed, relief palpable.

"And since we both seem to be alive and kickin,'" Danny continued, helping her to her feet. "That leads me to my next question."

He crossed his arms and stared down at her, concern suddenly morphing back into a furious scowl.

"What in the damn hell did you think you were doing?"

Keira blinked in surprise at the sudden shift in tone, far too taken aback to appeal to anything other than simple honesty.

"I-I thought, if I could find my way back, t-to where it started. I thought maybe . . . "

Danny stared at her as Keira's voice drifted away and her cheeks colored as she stared resolutely at her feet. When he finally spoke, his words were barely louder than a whisper.

"You thought you could get back."

Keira nodded silently, feeling heat flood her cheeks. She felt like a child, actually *worse* than a child. Because children didn't know better. She'd gotten herself into this mess, gotten *them* into this mess, and had no one to blame but herself. If Danny had gotten hurt, even—

Keira caught her breath, surprised by the sharp stabbing pain that struck her chest at the thought. She shook her head, banishing the images that she knew wouldn't soon abandon her nightmares.

Danny exhaled deeply, running a hand roughly through his hair.

"It doesn't work that way, Keira. It's not some magical portal. You were *brought* here. Didn't Elliott explain that?"

"Not really," Keira muttered. "I just . . . I had to be sure Danny." Keira looked up, eyes pleading for understanding. Danny searched her face and whatever he saw there made his expression soften incrementally.

"I get it," he said finally.

And somehow, impossibly, Keira believed him. She stared deep into his eyes, eyes that had moments ago been cold and murderous now seemed warm, like something she could melt into. Keira swallowed, suddenly very aware of how close they were standing but somehow unable to move away.

Neither spoke, the tension hanging between them like something alive, twisting and turning until Keira thought she'd break under the weight of it.

Danny was the first to cut through the tension with a soft chuckle.

"At this point, I'm honestly just shocked you let me ground you in the first place."

"Yeah, well," Keira muttered, rubbing the back of her neck and studiously avoiding his gaze. "Don't get used to it."

Danny laughed in earnest.

"Wouldn't dream of it, sweetheart."

Keira's head shot up and she opened her mouth for a scathing retort, but a thought suddenly caught her up short.

"How did you even find me, anyway?"

Danny's expression turned suddenly sheepish as he rubbed a hand across the back of his neck. "I—well, I could sort of sense you, I guess."

Keira blinked at him. "You could sense me?"

"Your pneuma, I mean." Danny added hastily. "When you tried to cast a bind on your own, my grounding energy just knew where to find you."

Danny shook his head and shrugged. "I don't really know how to explain it."

Keira bit her lip, fidgeting nervously with the hem of her tunic.

"So you can feel my pneuma when it's being cast out, find where I'm at. But that's it, right? This *connection* thing, it's not—it's not like, my *thoughts* or anything, right?"

Danny fixed her with a long inscrutable look and she searched his eyes nervously, feeling utterly exposed.

Finally, he swallowed thickly and nodded. "Just the pneuma."

Keira let out a breath she hadn't realized she'd been holding and considered this for a long moment. The old Keira would have been uncomfortable, alarmed even to have some odd spiritual connection definitely not of her choosing. But after everything that had happened, everything they'd been through . . .

She shrugged. "Well, I guess it's a good thing you did. Though I'd say your timing could use some work, O'Leary."

Danny rolled his eyes though she could see he was smiling in relief at her tone. Then a thought suddenly occurred to him and he grabbed her hand.

"Come with me, Altman."

CHAPTER

TWENTY-FIVE

"You said you had to see it, had to come back to where this all began."

Danny watched as Keira stared out at the roiling water. High above its usual height since the storm, branches and silt angrily churned amongst the eddies. Danny watched from the corner of his eye as Keira absently rubbed the broken locket between two fingers. He needed her to see it, to realize once and for all that there was no magical portal standing ready to bring her back to the life she knew.

Neither of them said a word, merely watching the water. Normally Danny would have felt impatient, would have demanded answers, filling the moment with unneeded words. But now he just felt . . . at peace.

It was Keira who spoke first.

"I—I don't know, Danny. I thought—" Keira's lips pressed into a thin line and Danny watched as the all-too familiar wrinkles formed between her brows. "I thought seeing it one more time would tell me . . . something. Thought I'd feel relief . . . or guilt. Just . . . something."

She shook her head and, to Danny's dismay, tears filled her eyes. Without thinking, he draped one arm over her shoulders, tugging her close until her head rested against him and one hand snuck around his waist.

She stared up at him, eyes gleaming, and the grief Danny saw there cut straight to his core.

"Does that make any sense at all?"

130

He nodded, because it did. Of course it did. How often had he sat on the banks of this very river recounting his days to his Ma.

"It's ok to miss her, Keira. Hell, I miss my own ma every day." He chuckled, rubbing a hand sheepishly against the back of his neck. But she didn't laugh.

"I—It's not just that, Danny. Sure, I miss her. But at the same time, I—I'm *happy* here.

"There's nothing wrong with staying, Keira. Starting a new life."

She shook her head. "You don't understand."

Danny fought down the rising frustration.

"Then explain it to me."

Keira shook her head, pulling away.

Danny grabbed her wrist, holding her in place.

"Keira, *please*. I just want to—"

"Because part of me wants to!" Keira cried, yanking her arm free before burying her face in her hands in a muffled sob. When she glanced up, her eyes were wide and filled with self-loathing.

"That same part of me that wanted so desperately to leave for college, to escape her and the life she made for us. I wanted more, I wanted better. I asked for space and I got it," Keira muttered quietly, shaking her head. "Boy, did I get it."

Danny stared at her, finally understanding.

"It's not your fault, Keira. You didn't ask for this. You didn't ask to die in a car accident, to leave your mother, and come here. None of this is your fault."

Eyes shining, Keira stared up at him with a look of such despair he thought his heart might actually break in two.

"Then why am I happy?" She whispered. "Why do I enjoy being here, training with Elliott, with Nazor, with . . . you?"

Danny swallowed, ignoring the warmth suddenly fluttering in his chest.

"You're making the best out of an awful situation." Danny whispered. Then hesitated a moment before adding, "It doesn't mean you love your ma any less."

Keira shook her head, staring out over at the river and once more fingering the broken locket he'd seen her clutch in nervous desperation so many times before.

"We don't choose the places we end up in this life, Keira. All we can do is try to create a good life with whatever rotten hand we're dealt. That's all any of us can do."

She was quiet for a long moment and Danny held his breath, hoping and praying she'd finally see sense. Finally, she sighed.

"I know you're right, O'Leary."

Danny grinned and opened his mouth to reply, but she beat him to it.

"I won't ever give up, though. Just so you know. On finding her, finding a way home. I owe her that much, at least."

Danny swallowed, fighting the sting of disappointment.

"Then the Legion is your best bet, Keira. Serving the Legion, fighting chaos, it's the best thing we could do for this world . . . and for our families. And then, well . . . maybe once our duty is fulfilled, they'll grant us both a way home."

Keira's face lit up at his words and she suddenly threw both arms around him, hugging him fiercely. He returned the hug instinctively, reveling in her warmth.

But when she pulled away to grin broadly up at him, he felt a twinge of guilt in his gut. He had no idea if there was a way home. Or what she would find if she actually made it there. He'd never heard of any Legionnaire achieving such a thing. But who knew? If anyone could do it, though, it would be the Legion. So it wasn't really a lie. Not really.

And time healed all wounds, right? In the face of eternity spent side by side, he didn't doubt that Keira's pain would fade as well.

They were partners, the two of them. That epic display of pneumonancy back in the clearing had proved as much.

They belonged together. He could see that now.

And someday, hopefully soon, Keira would as well.

TWENTY-SIX

Over the next couple of weeks, Keira did her absolute best to forget her idiotic runaway attempt and for the most part, life on the farm returned to some semblance of normal. She had been nervous as hell on the ride back from the river, fingers tapping relentlessly against the saddle until Danny accused her of making the horses angsty.

So she stopped.

And then started chewing her lip raw.

But she needn't have been so worried. Elliott and Nazor were waiting for them at the farm door. But upon seeing their battered and bruised faces, Elliott quickly ushered them inside, clucking over them like an anxious mother hen as he gathered his herbs and poultices.

Nazor said nothing, merely observed the proceedings with an unreadable expression. Keira did her best to avoid her gaze but the heat of those unwavering eyes seemed to burn through the top of her skull.

Finally, once they were cleaned and bandaged to Elliott's satisfaction, Keira could take the tension no longer. Steeling her spine, she met Nazor's gaze with her own unflinching stare and said,

"I'd like to return to training . . . if you'll have me."

Keira swallowed as Nazor merely stared back at her.

"How long do you plan on doing so?"

Keira couldn't help but flinch at the other woman's cool tone. But she quickly gritted her teeth and declared,

"As long as it takes. I'll pass the rites, become a Legionnaire. And then . . . well I guess I'll just have to see what comes after."

Nazor cocked her head slightly to the side, eyes searching Keira's for . . . something. Exactly what she couldn't say.

"We."

Keira's head snapped around to see that Danny had come to stand behind her. He took her hand, squeezing lightly as they both turned to face Elliott and Nazor.

"*We* will learn pneumonancy. *We* will pass the rites. And *we* will become legionnaires—whatever it takes."

Elliott clapped his hands together in delight, grinning broadly at the two of them. Nazor wasn't nearly so ebullient but Keira thought she saw a small smile tug at the corner of the woman's lips as she looked between the two of them.

"And so you shall . . . so you shall."

Since then, Keira and Danny had redoubled their training efforts, starting before dawn and not stopping until the last of the sun's rays filtered through the snow covered pines.

The training was much as it had always been, though now as soon as they'd utterly exhausted their bodies with sword craft, horseback riding, and hand to hand combat, they turned to pneumonancy and set about sapping their brains as well. Nazor and Elliott both pushed them pitilessly and every night Keira collapsed into bed, fast asleep before her head had barely hit the pillow.

Yet while she was exhausted, to be sure, she also felt . . . content. At peace in a way she'd rarely known since arriving in Loren. She had a purpose now, a goal. And Keira had always done her best work when a path was clearly laid before her.

Still, there were nights when the ache of homesickness smoldered in her chest and she'd have to find some excuse to leave. She'd venture out then. Not too far, but just beyond the prying eyes and overly sympathetic glances.

On one such night, dinner prepared, Keira ventured outside to join the horses. She breathed in the frigid night air as the chocolate mare nuzzled her arm. Cerise never looked at her differently, never questioned her or asked for more than she was willing to give. At that moment, Keira wanted nothing else.

Cerise nuzzled her gently in search of the carrots she knew she would find in her pockets. Keira smiled, quickly fishing one out.

"Keep feeding her like that, and you'll spoil her for sure." Nazor's voice came from over Keira's shoulder. Keira started at the noise and gripped the fence post to keep from toppling over. Nazor chuckled warmly.

"I'm sorry. I did not mean to distract you."

"No?" Keira asked, the weight of her annoyance buoyed by the sting of embarrassment.

Nazor didn't answer, merely sidling up to the railing. She stirred a steaming bowl of stew thoughtfully, obviously in no hurry to break the silence.

"You're doing well, you know."

Keira blinked at her in surprise. Nazor was definitely not one for compliments.

"Um . . . thank you."

Nazor merely nodded, eyes fixed on the horizon as she leaned against the fence. Keira returned to stroking Cerise's neck. She expected an awkwardness to fall in the silence between them. After all, she and Nazor had never exactly been close. But instead, the quiet that settled between them felt . . . warm.

To Keira's surprise, it was Nazor who broke the silence first.

"Do you still carry around that locket? The one that broke when you first arrived."

Keira blinked in surprise even as her hand moved to her pocket. She pulled out the locket and held it out.

"This one?"

Nazor nodded and began fishing into her own pockets.

She emerged with a small object that Keira had to step closer to see.

She gasped.

In Nazor's hand was an intricately braided band. Red, blue, and gold interwoven with such beautiful complexity that Keira couldn't help but stare.

"Three strands," Nazor said quietly. "One for Danny, one for Elliott, and one for me."

She held out her other hand and Keira wordlessly passed her the locket. Nazor deftly threaded the band through the clasp, before tying it securely around Keira's neck.

"Family is forever." Nazor murmured. "And though they may be gone, they will *never* be forgotten."

"It—it's beautiful." Keira breathed the words, admiring the intricate braid, the color of the threads set off beautifully by the gold of the locket.

"I have one just like it."

Keira glanced over to see Nazor running a similarly intricate bracelet between two fingers.

"Who—" Keira stopped herself before she said something insensitive, blushing as Nazor fixed her with a classically unreadable expression.

"My mother. My father. My—my daughter."

Nazor's voice cracked on the words and Keira's mouth fell open in surprise. She stared at her mentor, sure she must have misheard. She'd never seen or heard anything resembling brokenness from this pillar of a woman. Nazor was unbeatable, unbreakable, and impenetrable. She was made of stone, not a maternal bone in her body. But the woman standing before Keira now just looked . . . lost.

"I—I'm sorry."

Nazor nodded in acknowledgement. Keira, still reeling from this information, blurted out the only thing she could think of.

"How—I mean what, what happened?"

Nazor's brow furrowed as she stared out at the horses, bowl of stew all but forgotten in her hands.

"War."

Keira had nothing to say to that. But she needn't have worried. Because Nazor turned to her then and fixed her with a dagger-like stare.

"Our fight is not yet yours, Keira. Don't—" she held up a hand to silence the protest Keira had been about to utter. "Don't argue. It is only to be expected. Chaos, *true* chaos has not yet touched you, Keira. It has not slunk through in the dead of night and stolen the very people you care most about. But it will, Keira. One way or another. And it is then, when you have felt the sting of biting loss, that you shall truly be one of us. "

Keira opened her mouth to reply but shut it, for once, completely at a loss.

"These are dark and dangerous times, Keira. Chaos is looming, and we will need your strength if we are to see order restored."

She must have seen Keira's dubious expression because she quirked a small, indulgent smile her way.

"We do not choose the lot we are given, Keira. Chaos, order— either way, even the best-laid plans have a habit of unwinding."

Keira swallowed, no clue how to respond to that.

"But when that happens—"

Keira glanced up to see that Nazor was once more fixing her with a piercing gaze. The older woman reached out a hand and gripped her by the shoulder.

"When it happens, you will be ready. I will make you ready. You have my word."

Keira could only nod, watching as Nazor searched her face, praying she found whatever it was she was looking for, hoping she was enough.

Finally, Nazor straightened and nodded brusquely, her inspection clearly completed.

"Come now. Your dinner is no doubt getting cold. That is, if Danny hasn't already devoured it whole."

They both chuckled at that because Keira had zero doubt in her mind that Danny would indeed eat her dinner rather than let it go to waste, partners or no.

But still she hesitated.

"I'll be just a minute."

Nazor nodded and turned toward the house. Keira once more looked down at the locket and band. She rubbed a finger across the cool surface and squeezed her eyes shut against the tears that threatened.

"I'll never forget, Mom. I promise. There are some things I have to do here. But I promise, some how, some way, I'll make it home to you."

At her words, there was a whistle of wind that coursed through the forest. Keira shivered, watching as the tall, bare oak trees that rimmed that paddock swayed heavily against the breeze. And she was left feeling . . . full.

She turned then back to the farmhouse and the newfound family that awaited her there.

CHAPTER

TWENTY-SEVEN

Several months later, Keira found Danny mucking out the stables and sidled up to lean against the doorframe, watching him. She said nothing, and he didn't press her, content to work silently under her measuring gaze.

He's a good one, Keira decided, watching him pause to offer a treat to the horses. She didn't know much, but she knew that Danny O'Leary had a truly good heart. She couldn't say precisely why, but she knew that for certain.

"You planning on helping or just gawking?"

Keira started, blushing as she hurried out of the stable entrance. He still hadn't looked up from his chores but his lips pressed into a thin line that looked suspiciously like a smile.

"Oh, but you're doing *such* a good job." Keira grinned as she hopped up onto the nearby stall. She forced her voice into a very serious timber before adding, "I would just *hate* to be in the way."

Danny snorted but stopped to reach for a nearby rag. He dragged it across his gleaming face, still not looking at her. Keira's eyes narrowed in suspicion and she opened her mouth to—

Spinning, Danny threw the balled up sweaty rag directly at her face with a speed better suited to Fenway park.

Keira squealed, toppling off the stall door in an attempt to dodge the rag. She landed in an unceremonious heap on the stable floor.

Danny was bent over, clutching his stomach and wiping tears from his eyes as he belly laughed.

138

Keira scowled back at him but even she couldn't help a snort of amusement.

"Yeah yeah yeah. Very funny."

"Sorry," he said, offering her a hand. "I just had a flashback to your first sparring attempt."

Keira sputtered with outrage before promptly kicking his legs out from under him.

Danny fell to the ground beside her with a loud whoop . They both laid there for a long moment, trying to catch their breath as peals of laughter echoed around the stable.

"We'll make a fighter out of you yet, Altman."

Keira rolled her eyes. "Well, it can't be any worse than my sword-craft," she said. Danny nodded, considering.

"That's fair. You *are* pretty terrible."

Keira shoved him, gasping in outrage as they both laughed.

They were interrupted by the sound of galloping hoofbeats and quickly scrambled to their feet.

They emerged from the stable to see Nazor jumping from her black destrier, clearly just arriving from the road to town.

She glanced up as they headed toward her, a grim look on her face. Elliott appeared in the farmhouse doorway and hurried toward them.

"The baker's son, Errol, was accosted on the southern road, held up by thieves claiming to be lawmen sent to collect the baker's unpaid taxes. They beat the poor lad within an inch of his life."

Keira gaped at her. "That's horrible!" She glanced at Danny and even he looked shocked.

Nazor shook her head, turning then to Elliott. "I doubt they acted alone."

They both gazed at each other for a long moment, a silent conversation clearly occurring. Finally, Nazor spoke aloud. "First the portents, the sickness among the animals and the trees, then Keira's attack, the rebel activity to the South, and now this—" Nazor shook her head. "The chaos we've long foreseen is finally here. I think it's time. We should send word to the Legion."

Keira's eyes shot to Danny, brows raised. But he wasn't looking at her.

"You think this is more than highway bandits, don't you." Danny's words were quiet and held no question. Nazor and Elliott glanced at each other before turning to Keira and Danny.

Elliott nodded, considering. His mouth was set in a thin line, and his eyes looked wary. "Indeed. It would seem that the rising unrest has finally reached Abalás. I don't think the Legion can stay out of this any longer."

A well of excitement ballooned in Keira's chest and she had to fight the smile that slowly spread across her face. This was it. This was her chance. All of this training finally had a purpose. The Legion was coming and she would finally get the chance to prove herself.

Join the cause. Fight the chaos. Make it home.

Whatever it took, she would not fail. Not this time.

CHAOS LOOMING

CHAPTER ONE

In the silence of the moonlit forest, all seemed to be in order. Yet the cord of chaos thrummed beneath, heard only by those who cared to listen.

Keira Altman felt that cord in her bones and let its steady pulse ground her. She breathed in the air, thick with anticipation, as the legionnaires creeped through the underbrush, their footsteps light on the dew-laden leaves of the forest floor. Bringing up the rear, Keira followed suit. Barely daring to breathe, her legs moved double time to keep up with the others' loping strides.

When they'd crested the hill, she finally glanced up, sucking air through her teeth at the sight before her. Even in the dead of night, Marek Larghaen's manor cast a pall over the single-story wattle and daub buildings that gathered at the base of the hill, making up the small fishing village of Abalás. The shadow of the tax collector's extravagance stretched menacingly out over its surroundings.

Keira swallowed, refusing to let the others see the nerves that coiled like a nest of vipers in her belly, the way her traitorous limbs threaten to shake. No, she'd asked to be here, pleaded even. She'd been desperate to join this mission despite her mentor Nazor's protests that she was far too inexperienced. Well here she was, creeping around in the pitch black outside the house of possibly the most dangerous man in the uplands. She'd gotten exactly what she'd wanted. Now if only she could keep from screwing it up.

A hissed warning from the lead legionnaire shocked her out of her reverie. He'd dropped to his knees and was gesturing for them to follow suit. Keira dove for the nearest bush, heart pounding and unsheathed blade at the ready. She didn't dare move, instead listening hard for the source of the delay. A movement to her right caught her eye and she saw Danny motioning toward the manor. She inched around the shrubbery just in time to see a flickering candle disappear from the window.

She glanced at Danny, his pale green eyes just visible over the dark mask that covered his mouth and nose. They tightened in silent question and Keira shook her head. She couldn't imagine why anyone would be awake at this hour. In fact, their entire plan hinged on the element of surprise.

What if the old snake had been warned? The corrupt merchant had enough spies—helpless people indebted to him and willing to do anything to escape his grasp. What if they were walking into a trap? Keira squeezed her eyes shut, forcing her breathing to slow as she focused all her attention on the here and now.

You can do this, she reminded herself. Over a year of endless training and she was as ready as she'd ever be. No, this was her shot—maybe her only chance to be admitted to the rites that year. And if she became a full legionnaire . . . well maybe, just maybe, she'd finally find a way home.

Home.

The thought sent a ripple of excitement down her spine and sparked a flame of yearning deep in her gut. Without consciously thinking, her hand went to the gold locket she always wore around her neck—the one her mother had given her on the last day they'd been together. But that was in a world far away from this one—a world filled with everyday miracles like electricity and refrigeration. It had been over a year since her life had been turned upside down—since she'd lost everything and everyone she cared about. Well, this new world had given her a second chance, and she'd be dammed if she let that happen again. Turns out dying has a way of bringing out your determined side.

Danny's quick head jerk brought her back to reality and she creeped her head around the shrubs to see the two lead legionnaires crouched together, heads bent in whispered consultation. Keira's heart thudded a quick staccato.

Would they turn back? There'd be no shame in that. Even though she'd volunteered for this raid, if it ended in retreat, no one could blame her. Sure the rites would remain just outside her grasp, but so too would the humiliation sure to follow if she failed her first true test.

But before she could think herself in any more circles, the lead legionnaire rose to his feet, motioning them forward once again. They continued their slow progress up the hill, one by one, stepping carefully to avoid the loudest patches of underbrush. Keira watched as the other black-clad figures slipped off in pairs, each going to their assault points. A light brush on her arm brought her attention back to Danny, who nodded toward the cellar door at the rear of the lodge. Reminded of their assignment, Keira took a deep breath, steeling herself for the task ahead.

Come on, Altman, don't screw this up.

They reached the cellar doors all too soon and Keira glanced around nervously, scanning for guards who might come to investigate their activities. Danny tried the door handle gingerly, then more forcefully. As they'd guessed, it was latched from the other side. He turned to her expectantly.

Time for Plan B.

Keira wiped her sweaty palms on her trousers, fiddling with the mask that covered her face as her eyes darted around the clearing. Danny's brow furrowed.

"You all right?" He asked, the Boston Irish lilt of his voice barely above a whisper.

Keira nodded, not trusting her voice to come out any stronger than a squeak—not exactly the tone of confidence she'd hoped to convey.

She forced her leaden legs to move as she kneeled before the cellar door. A warm squeeze on her shoulder made her glance up to meet Danny's warm gaze. He gave her a small nod and she felt something warm and gooey fill her insides, filling and soothing the gouges her fear had carved into her in the way only Danny could. There was a reason he was her grounder after all.

She could do this.

She took a deep breath and turned back to the cellar door, feeling Danny move into position to guard her back. She'd be royally screwed if someone tried to sneak up on her once she began the binding process—not the way she hoped to end the night, or her short second life.

Reaching deep inside herself, Keira gently nudged the mass of energy that lay just behind her stomach. Sending it downward through her feet, she firmly anchored herself to the grassy patch she'd chosen. Then, reaching out for the latch, she let the energy flow through her fingers as her lips puckered in a whistle. Called pneuma, or "breath," she knew the energy was too high for normal ears to detect. She felt this energy being twisted and shaped to match the waves of sound, and she altered the pitch of her note, letting it guide the pneuma into the shape she needed—wrought iron. All materials, and even people, had a shape to their pneuma, an amplitude and frequency to the energy holding them together. While a person's pneuma could change over time, the pneuma of objects like this lock remained a constant, unalterable touchstone.

She willed her pneuma to first match the iron's, then alter slightly, slowly disrupting its tidy molecular structure. The latch felt cold in her hand as it pulled the heat from her body, disordering the molecules that comprised it until the metal was nothing more than a molten blob. Wiping the sweat from her brow, Keira grasped the ledge of the door, easing it upward until the metal bindings gave way with a dull *thunk*. Below them stretched earthen steps that led down into the cellar.

Danny began descending the stairs, longsword at the ready. They'd decided he'd go in first, to stall for time should they encounter anyone, and to give her the space to orchestrate a binding if needed. Following close behind, Keira nearly ran smack into Danny, as he he froze at the bottom of the steps. She halted, listening for the sound that had caught his attention.

Bringing a finger to his lips, Danny inched forward again, deeper into the dank caverns of the cellar. Keira gripped the hilt of her sword and balled her left hand into a fist to hide its shaking.

You can do this. Just keep moving forward.

They were almost to the far end of the cellar now, and Keira could just make out the outline of the promised ladder leading to the main floor above. She barely registered the creak of a door hinge before something slammed her against the wall, sending her sword flying. She dropped to the ground, breath ragged as she tried to keep from heaving onto the floor.

She shoved aside what looked like a chair and scrambled to her feet. Hearing Danny cursing nearby, and the clang of metal as he fought off his own seemingly more human assailant, she staggered forward.

Keira emerged into a filthy larder to see him locked hilt to hilt with one of the conniving Marek Larghaen's hired men. She swore under her breath. They'd hoped to catch him unawares, but it seemed the old bastard had been warned, and had upped his guard to prepare for their arrival.

Keira sprinted toward Danny, shouting his name. His gaze shot up and with a great *umph,* spun the man he'd been grappling with in her direction just as she reached them. She met his back with her blade and felt an unsettling *crunch* as it slid through him. The man slumped against her, and she briefly bore his weight before letting him slide to the ground. He gurgled blood as Keira pulled her sword from his back, then was still.

"You okay?" Danny asked, quickly scanning her up and down.

Keira nodded. She couldn't seem to look away from the man at her feet. He was definitely dead—his eyes had that blank, dilated look that corpses get and he smelled like he'd wet himself. Her mentor, Elliott, had told her the end wasn't pretty, but until this moment, she hadn't fully grasped the horror that would be her first kill. She swallowed hard, avoiding Danny's eyes. She wasn't ready for the understanding and sympathy she knew she'd find there.

Blinking furiously, Keira forced her gaze away from the body. "Fine," she muttered. "You?"

"I'll live."

She knew he wanted to say more, knew the moment he thought better of it. She was grateful for that—Danny always seemed to know exactly what she needed.

"We should keep moving," Danny said. "On account of it seems like the others have run into trouble too. We need to get to Marek before he pulls off another of his grand escapes."

Keira nodded, noticing for the first time the sounds of fighting echoing from elsewhere in the lodge. She wadded up her confusing mix of emotions and flung them to the back of her mind. She'd have time to deal with them later. Peering around for an exit, Keira noted that the larder had seen better days. A thick layer of dust and grease covered the chopping tables and cabinetry, but the still-smoldering embers in the grand fireplace betrayed the room's recent use.

Shouts and curses echoed from the front rooms, but Keira and Danny instead headed for the servants' staircase in the back of the larder. The steps creaked as they swiftly climbed, making for the bedchambers on the floor above. But when an echoing creak reached their ears, they both froze. Any sound was amplified in the tight quarters and Keira barely dared to breathe as the creaking grew closer and closer. Her eyes darted to Danny's to find he'd pressed himself against the far wall, one finger pressed to his lips. Keira similarly eased herself flat against the wall opposite and forced air through her nostrils. *Inhale*. The creaking was just around the corner now. *Exhale*. Keira and Danny leaped forward, swords at the ready.

Tiny squeals and muffled sobs met them as a woman dressed only in a sleeping shift pressed two small children to her.

"Please, oh please," the woman cried. "They're just children. A- and I'm their nursemaid."

Danny was the first to step forward, brandishing a torch from the wall as he quickly surveyed the woman. Her dress was plain enough and she didn't appear to be hiding any weapons, making her story seem plausible.

"What do you think, Keira?" Danny asked. "I wasn't aware Marek had any kids, personally."

Keira didn't answer, throat working silently as her eyes fixed on the two small children. The smallest was a boy, no more than two or three whose sandy brown hair stuck up at odd ends. Fat crocodile tears filled his eyes as he stared up at her and he quickly buried his face in his nursemaid's skirts. But his sister, only a few years older from the looks of it didn't cry but stared wide-eyed at Keira as if transfixed. Her blonde hair was neatly parted with braids framing her face on either side. *Just like Molly*.

"We should see them out," Keira said suddenly. She didn't know where the impulse came from, but once uttered it just felt *right*. She couldn't leave them.

"There isn't time." Danny hissed. "They'll be fine."

But she shook her head and thought about the man and dog they'd encountered in the cellar. There could be more. Staring at the wide-eyed children all she could see was Molly, the little sister who wasn't even truly related to her, and the car accident that meant she may never see her again. But this little girl was here, now, and she'd be damned if she let anything happen to her.

"There could be fighting outside," she whispered back at him. "I have to make sure they make it safely."

"The mission—"

"I'll catch up to you," Keira insisted, sliding one hand into the girl's trembling one as she led the three of them down the steps.

From behind, she heard Danny's whispered curse. But there was no time to worry about that. They were innocent, these three, caught up in something they likely could never understand. She'd been there, silently begging for help from strangers who merely averted their gaze from the uncomfortable or inconvenient. She would never be that person.

It took only a few minutes to see the children and their nursemaid safely out through the cellar—their path thankfully absent any unexpected encounters. When Keira returned to take the stairs two at a time, she nearly ran smack into Danny and swore in surprise.

"Y-you stayed." *Obviously*, she chided herself.

Danny steadied her with one hand, meeting her gaze with a single cocked eyebrow.

"Now when've I eva' left you behind?"

Keira flushed and could only offer a half-hearted shrug. He was right, of course. Danny was nothing if not steadfast and loyal to a fault. He'd sooner have chewed off his own arm than left her back unguarded. It was the thing she loved most about him.

That thought sent a warm tingly sensation all the way to her toes and Keira felt her blush deepen. Now was *definitely* not the time for such thinking.

Luckily Danny had already turned and continued their ascent up the back staircase. Keira hurried after him, hand tightening on the hilt of her sword as she forced herself to refocus. They paused when they reached the landing, and Keira motioned toward a room on their left, where candlelight flickered beneath the closed door. Someone was definitely inside.

They flanked the door, one on either side, and Danny raised his eyebrows at her expectantly. She closed her eyes and concentrated on the pneuma. Slowly, Keira cast it out on the back of an inaudible whistle, searching with her mind for the presence they sought. The pneuma she encountered was twisted, dark, and calculating, but tinged with something else—a nervous tension of sorts. It was definitely Marek, all right, but he wasn't alone.

She could feel him pacing on the other side of the door along with two others, most likely bodyguards. Coming back to herself, she caught Danny's eye and held up three fingers. His brow furrowed. They'd been told Marek had only one bodyguard he trusted to share a room with him as he slept, and the original plan had been for her to muscle bind Marek while Danny took care of the bodyguard. Two guards threw that notion out the window, as she could only cast one bind at a time, and the out-of-body requirements of casting made her useless in a physical fight. That's why Danny was there—to guard her back during the process, and to help bring her back if she lost control. This would be difficult for him to do while fighting off two assailants at once.

She shook her head, and he nodded in response. Though the mask covered half his face, she knew he was grimacing underneath. They'd have to do this the old-fashioned way.

Danny grasped the door's handle while Keira mimed the general location of each of the three targets. Her fingers counted them down. *Three*...her grip tightened on the hilt of her sword...*two*...Danny's calm, determined eyes met hers...*one!*

With a shove, Danny flung open the door and rushed the closest bodyguard. Quick on his heels, Keira sprinted into the room and slammed into the other, meeting his sword with the clang of her own. She cursed their rotten luck—of course they had their weapons at the ready. No doubt they could hear the shouts echoing from the rest of the house.

She didn't have time to think about this long before she felt her sword drawn up and around in a giant arc, disentangling their blades and putting her immediately on the defensive. She barely blocked a crushing overhead swing. *This must be Rhondor*, she thought. *Marek's favorite.* Panic welled within her. *He's too big.*

She quickly squashed the panicked thought and forced herself to think rationally. *This is what you've trained for.* The man was enormous, and the broadsword he wielded nearly doubled his arm's reach. She needed to get some distance, or he'd skewer her for sure. After parrying his next slash, Keira snatched up a ceramic plate from the table behind her. When Rhondor advanced again, she blocked his stroke while simultaneously shattering the plate against his head. He stumbled backward, allowing her a few precious seconds to regain her bearings.

From the corner of her eye, she saw a huddled figure creep along the edge of the room, making for the open hall door.

Oh, no you don't, she thought.

Shifting her sword into her left hand, using the other to snatch up her hip dagger and sent it flying end over end into Marek's side. The man cried out and doubled over in pain.

Keira grinned in satisfaction. *That'll keep him from getting too far.*

Before she could revel in her minor victory, Rhondor was on her again, and he was angrier than ever. Keira, remembering everything her mentor Nazor had ever taught her, spun out of his way, letting his momentum carry him into the wall behind. As she turned, she brought her blade down in a sweeping arc, slicing the giant man collar to navel. It wasn't a deep cut—certainly not mortal—but it was enough to slow his movements as he forced her back on the defensive, hammering her with slashes and stabs. He was tiring, but so was Keira. Her breathing was shallow, and her sword felt heavier with every block.

Rhondor's wound was bleeding freely now, forming a small pool at his feet. Sensing an opportunity, Keira retreated slightly. Rhondor immediately pressed his advantage and leaped toward her, his foot slipping on his own blood. He didn't fall, but he definitely stumbled.

That was all Keira needed.

She lunged forward, cutting a single stroke in and up, wedging her blade between the giant's ribs. He exhaled sharply, then dropped to his knees, blood bubbling past his lips. She let him sag to the floor, then wrenched her blade free and spun to look for Danny.

He was in the opposite corner of the room, dealing the final blow to the other guard, a savage slice to the man's neck that left him in a gurgling heap. Danny turned toward her, and she saw a cruel cut down the side of his left arm. She started forward, brows knit with concern, but he waved her off.

"Just a scratch," Danny reassured her.

She nodded, not entirely convinced, but knew better than to argue just then.

"Where's Marek?" Danny asked.

Keira glanced around and cursed. "Well, he can't have gone far, not with my knife sticking out of his gut."

She saw a ghost of a smile cross Danny's face as he ran for the door. Out in the hallway, he bent to look at something on the floor before motioning her closer.

"Definitely blood. Seems you're not quite as hopeless at knife-throwing as Nazor says," he teased.

Keira scowled. "I told you I hit him. Honestly, I'm surprised he made it this far. From what they told us, I didn't take him for much of a fighter. His type always seems to have others around for the dirty work."

Danny's smile twisted darkly. "Never underestimate the survival instincts of a man like Marek. He didn't get to where he's at for lack of determination."

Keira nodded, gritting her teeth. She'd never met Marek Larghaen, but she knew enough about the snake to suspect that Danny was probably right. The slimy merchant had clambered over the backs of his fellow uplanders to become the local Tiarna's chief tax collector, keeping his power through threats, intimidation, and outright violence. *Yes*, Keira thought grimly, *he was certainly motivated, but that makes two of us.*

A clatter of metal hitting the floor brought their attention to a room at the far end of the hall. The two of them slipped down the hall toward the sound, careful to check each room they passed to ensure they wouldn't be ambushed. As they approached the far door, Keira heard voices coming from inside—laughing, it sounded like. Danny pressed his ear to the door, a puzzled look on his face, then sighed in relief.

Throwing open the door, he and Keira entered to find a cowering Marek, surrounded by four of their fellow Legionnaires. Though masks obscured their faces, Keira quickly recognized their mentors, Elliott and Nazor.

"Nice of you both to join us," Nazor growled.

~

The story continues in *Chaos Looming,* in stores now!

About the Author

H.B. Reneau is an author of fantasy and contemporary fiction. Author, physician, and proud dog mom, she is known for her character-driven, genre-crossing fiction that draws on her experiences in both medicine and the military. She has a particular love for strong female characters who face up to adversity and manage to subvert some expectations along the way.

To learn more, head over to her website at www.hbreneau.com. There you'll find her books, blog, and fun extras. Or reach out directly! Follow on social media and sign up for the monthly newsletter to receive receive free gifts, awesome discounts, and updates on all her latest projects.

If you enjoyed this book, please consider leaving a review at your favorite online storefront!

ALSO BY H.B. RENEAU

The Legion of Pneumos

Chaos Looming

Haven Enduring

The Legion of Pneumos: Novella Collection

The Cantor

The Centus

The Rebel

The Remnant

www.ingramcontent.com/pod-product-compliance
Lightning Source LLC
Chambersburg PA
CBHW032032180726
48284CB00008B/2555